Praise for *Fugitive Blue*

'Claire Thomas's *Fugitive Blue* is a fine first novel about the search by a young art conservator to find the origins of a fifteenth-century panel painting. In narratives about different historical periods, from Renaissance Venice through to post-war Australia, Thomas suggests parallel stories about love and loss, female creativity and unrealised desire. Polished and poignant, expressed with incisiveness and resonance, *Fugitive Blue* doesn't miss a beat.' *Westerly*

'Intricately structured, written with originality and poise... *Fugitive Blue* is a novel about art, the fragility of love and transformation. The fresh and vivid images evoked resonate with the reader long after the novel is finished.' Judges for the Dobbie Literary Award

'Written with élan and delightful ease... Thomas captures atmosphere with artful economy and sketches characters and emotions with masterly precision. A novel to be reckoned with.' Murray Waldren

'... beautifully done with great imagination.' *Sydney Morning Herald*

'... beautifully written, elegant and very enjoyable...' *Launceston Examiner*

'Reminiscent of Tracy Chevalier's *Girl with a Pearl Earring*, this novel is an elegantly written work that interweaves the past and the present...' *Sun-Herald*

'... a strong sense of historical time and place presented through the beautifully descriptive passages... well-written with excellent characters... Its interesting subject matter has been intelligently interwoven within a multi-layered story of love lost, past and present and the endurance of art. It will appeal to an unlimited range of readers...' *Bookseller & Publisher*

'... immediately enticing...' *Canberra Times*

'A captivating novel about the fragility and essence of love. Indeed it is a work of art.' *Gold Coast Bulletin*

'... beguiling debut novel...' *Sunday*

FUGITIVE
BLUE

Also by Claire Thomas

The Performance

FUGITIVE BLUE

CLAIRE THOMAS

Quoted material: *p. v*: Dawson W. Carr and Mark Leonard (eds), *Looking at Paintings—A Guide to Technical Terms*, published by J Paul Getty Museum, Malibu, a division of British Museum Publications Ltd, London, 1992, p. 33; Johann Wolfgang von Goethe, *Theory of Colours*, translated by Charles Lock Eastlake, MIT Press, Cambridge, 1970, p. 311; A.S. Byatt, *Possession*, Random House (Vintage), London, 1991, p. 169; *p. 63*: Guy Chapman (ed.), *The Travel-Diaries of William Beckford of Fonthill*, Constable/Houghton Mifflin, London, 1928, p. 78; *p. 110*: Tennessee Williams, *A Streetcar Named Desire and Other Plays*, Penguin, London, 1959, p. 162; *p. 113*: Emile Zola, *The Masterpiece*, translated by Thomas Watson and Roger Pearson, Oxford University Press, Oxford, 1999, p. 41; *pp. 158–9*: Samuel Beckett, *Waiting for Godot*, Faber & Faber, London, 1965, p. 33; *p. 163*: George Seferis, 'Five Poems by Mr S. Thalassinos', in Keeley, Edmund, Sherrard, Philip; *George Seferis: Collected Poems*, Princeton University Press, 1967, 1995 revised edition, p. 59; *p. 206*: Stella Bowen, *Drawn from Life*, London: Virago, 1984, p. 168.

First published by Allen & Unwin in 2008

Published in Australia and New Zealand in 2021
by Hachette Australia
(an imprint of Hachette Australia Pty Limited)
Level 17, 207 Kent Street, Sydney NSW 2000
www.hachette.com.au

10 9 8 7 6 5 4 3 2 1

 A catalogue record for this
book is available from the
National Library of Australia

ISBN: 978 0 7336 4534 1 (paperback)

Cover design by Alissa Dinallo
Cover photograph courtesy of Shutterstock
Text design by Bookhouse
Typeset by Bookhouse
Printed and bound in Australia by McPherson's Printing Group

The paper this book is printed on is certified against the Forest Stewardship Council® Standards. McPherson's Printing Group holds FSC® chain of custody certification SA-COC-005379. FSC® promotes environmentally responsible, socially beneficial and economically viable management of the world's forests.

Dedicated with love to
Cheryl Thomas

'Fugitive pigment: a pigment that is particularly susceptible to changing over time.'

DAWSON W. CARR AND MARK LEONARD, EDS,
Looking at Paintings—A Guide to Technical Terms

'But as we readily follow an agreeable object that flies from us, so we love to contemplate blue, not because it advances to us, but because it draws us after it.'

GOETHE, *Theory of Colours*

'It may be that your diligent—reconstitution—like the restoration of old Frescoes with new colours—is our way to the Truth—a discreet patching.'

A.S. BYATT, *Possession*

I

I am not writing this to be sentimental. I am just trying to find the answer to a story.

I did not imagine myself here. I certainly did not imagine myself here alone. So, for you and for myself, I want to explain how it happened. How this bit of it happened, anyway. Because there are other threads, of course, that I cannot find, that twist and pull at me now and will probably continue to do so forever.

But with you, there is no forever. Of course. I am away from home so it is more difficult to comprehend that, harder than it would be if I were in Melbourne where we lived. Or in Asia, where you are now. But I'm here, instead, in this old wet European city, and so I must repeat some words over and over to myself to comprehend. No forever. Slowly, I am beginning to register it.

This is the part I'm telling you.

❧

There was nothing unusual about the arrival of Ana Poulos. She walked into the Centre like the other clients, then waited in the foyer for a few minutes, sitting neatly on a charcoal upholstered bench. The senior conservators were at a conference that morning, so I had been asked to greet her. I squeaked down the dark rubber floor of the passage towards the client, roughly wiping my hands on my black apron before pushing through the heavy transparent door of the foyer.

She stood up, held out her hand and I welcomed her.

'Let's go into the meeting room,' I said.

She was carrying a leather handbag that pulled at the red sleeve covering her forearm and a brown paper bag, the type you get from clothing stores, with crisp side folds and twisted cord handles. Her bags bounced together as we moved towards the consultation table that dominated the meeting room in the Centre. As I followed Ana Poulos, I tried to see what was inside the paper bag—to make out a shape or a sense of weight—but the only visible detail was a small corner of white tissue poking out at the top.

'You can put it up here,' I suggested.

With that, she placed her things on the table and pushed the handbag to one side. Then she pulled a work of art from the brown paper bag, releasing a few unexpected flakes of paint like shaken-off snow. I followed a piece of it as it floated into a dimple of rubber between our two pairs of feet. Ana's black court shoes, my grey Campers and a dot of blue between them. I had to stop myself from rushing through to the lab and grabbing a container to collect the delicate debris.

Mrs Poulos folded back the tissue paper and there it was. A simple composition. Two fat angels flying through blue, white wings waving and little legs kicking out behind.

'Wow.'

'It belonged to my mother,' Ana explained. 'She recently passed away.'

'I'm sorry,' I said. And then I felt my face heating up. Five minutes into the consultation and I'd already hit a moment in which my awkward words got stuck.

'That's okay,' she smiled. 'She was over ninety.'

I tried to be professional. 'This looks like it could date from the early Renaissance, perhaps the mid-fifteenth century. It could be a practice piece by a workshop apprentice. Does that fit with what you know?'

'I don't know much at all about its history, really.'

'See that knot in the wood there,' I continued, waving my smudge-covered fingers over the painting. 'That would have been enough for it to be rejected by a professional. And the subject's unusual.'

'The angels?'

'Yes. Angels are everywhere now but in this period they were usually placed on the edge of the picture. Like fruit or leaves. As an embellishment.'

Mrs Poulos nodded. 'I've often thought of it as a draft for something larger. Like a study in a sketchbook?'

'Maybe,' I said. 'But it is properly finished. And all that blue. It looks like ultramarine. Ultramarine wouldn't have been used in a study.'

'The pigment?'

'Yes. It was very expensive, literally worth more than its weight in gold at certain times. It comes from lapis lazuli, the gemstone.'

'Oh yes,' she said. 'I've got a lapis pendant.' And then she reached inside her red shirt and pulled out a smooth sphere of blue, held to a long chain by thin tentacles of gold. 'I've had this since the seventies.'

'It's lovely,' I said. And I thought of my own lapis jewellery: beads of flecked stone I'd bought from Ishka as a teenager. I'd forgotten what I'd done with those bracelets. Probably just shoved them inside some box with countless other discarded decorations. Friendship bands plaited from embroidery thread, brightly coloured badges for radio station promos, a few sparkling pink hairclips.

'Isn't it interesting how the value of things can change so much?' Mrs Poulos said. 'What's considered precious at various times through history.'

I nodded my agreement, remembering a limestone Romanesque Madonna who was a chameleon over epochs. Initially painted black, the thirteenth century had seen her coated blue in recognition of the newfound significance of that hue. Later, she was given a Baroque revamp—gilded in gaudy gold—before being consumed, two centuries later, by lashings of white in a chilly response to a new doctrinal notion of purity. And I thought of the apothecaries I'd learnt about in art history with their hidden stash of ultramarine treasure and then the woven shop basket I'd fumbled through as a thirteen-year-old, tugging my chosen blue bracelets from a tangled mass of beaded colour.

'Well, do you think you'll be able to restore this?' Mrs Poulos asked, getting to the point of it all.

'We can definitely try,' I replied. 'I might not do the work personally, but the Centre would be happy to take it on. There's no doubt about that.'

My instructions that morning had been simple. Accept anything that looks like it could benefit from conservation treatment, explain the general procedural and fee options, and reassure the client that all due care would be taken with her possession.

As soon as Mrs Poulos left the Centre, I dashed into the lab, grabbed a small glass beaker and a pair of tweezers, returned to the meeting room and rescued five flakes of blue paint: the fragment from the floor and the others from across the table. Then I sat down and stared at the patch of colour that had just landed on an expanse of beige laminate. I was excited by my proximity to what was possibly one of the oldest artworks to have arrived at the Centre. I secured my hair back into a ponytail and leant forward on the table, my elbows resting on its surface as I scrutinised the painting.

It was more of a plank than a standard joined panel—just a single piece of wood, coarsely sawn with the cuts still splintered. It had been previously restored, probably during the nineteenth century: a cradle support was attached to its back in an attempt to prevent the timber from curling and twisting as a reminder that it had once belonged to the trunk of a tree. The painting covered the surface with only a thin border of exposed wood left bare around the edges. There was significant degradation in the paint layers with visible cracking and flaking. It was unvarnished. The blue was still vibrant, although typically faded. The angels were united, complementary, but also unusually idiosyncratic: one was confidently cheeky with an almost coquettish tilt to its fleshy neck, the other a classic, wide-eyed innocent with a ruddier complexion and grasping, extended arms. Thick golden curls adorned their heads. Their plump legs were discreetly positioned to obscure any genitalia, while their faces had a pretty gender ambivalence. Their wings. Their wings were full of air, exultant. The brushwork was inconsistent—

Suddenly there was a thud at the doorway as my boss powered in to inspect what had been received in her absence. Gillian walked towards me, rolling up her long knitted sleeves. She leant over my shoulder towards the object on the table.

'Wow,' she said. 'What the *hell* is this?'

That was the beginning.

❧

Later that night, when I got home to our flat, I thought I'd try to find my old lapis lazuli hippy bracelets. I sat down on the floor in the study and began to pull out the piles of belongings stored behind the big sliding doors of the built-in wardrobe. Everything stank. It reminded me of when you'd put on a t-shirt that had been left sitting in the washing machine too long, so that the dampness had settled into the fibres and remained there even after the fabric was dry. The wardrobe had that mildew whiff without your masking cologne. As I pulled out box after box, the odour became increasingly pronounced.

The objects were slightly damp, then sodden, then, finally, as the bottom layer of boxes was uncovered, soaking wet. Everything inside the wardrobe was mine; you'd never stored anything in there. A shoebox I must've had for almost fifteen years was so drenched that it disintegrated at my touch; a sketch of a sneaker in profile evolved into a spongy pulp and several blocks of paper tumbled out. I cradled the dripping clumps as ink seeped into my hands. I was holding a pile of photographs, transformed into smears of colour with the images sticking together in stacks. I tried to peel the pictures apart and locate a discernible portion but all I found was a glimpse of a landscape, a hint of a hair ribbon.

The notations I'd earnestly written on the reverse side of the photographs were mostly illegible. I dropped the mess back inside the remains of the storage box; there was a muffled splat like a tomato landing in a sink.

Eventually, after carefully arranging the wet objects on a few old towels, I did find the jewellery that had initiated my search. I retrieved the blue beads from inside a hard green plastic box and shoved one bracelet onto my adult arm. It stretched tightly over my wristwatch.

The floor inside the wardrobe was wet. Plaster crumbs from the back wall covered the carpet and the melamine shelving was exposed—warped and tenuous. I sat there, feeling oddly desolated, with those drenched boxes of childhood archives encircling me like gravestones. Persistent spots of white—paint, plaster, paper?—clung to my dark clothing like lint.

I was devastated by what I'd found. How ridiculous that seems now. A few ruined letters from penpals and destroyed happy snaps. But then, I couldn't cope. Imagine: that water frightened and confused me. I got up and left the room I'd already renamed. I shut the door on the Rotting Room, grateful that you were not going to be home for a fortnight.

೬

The following day at work, I was required to make a call to Ana Poulos to get more detailed information about her panel painting and its history.

'It's important for us to determine the provenance,' I explained to her. 'So we know as much as possible about the conditions the artwork has been subjected to.'

She was very patient with my inquiries, telling me the few facts that she knew. The painting had belonged to her mother and, prior to that, her mother's French grandmother who had lived in Paris before moving to Greece with her husband. That was the extent of her knowledge. Mrs Poulos was unaware of any existing documentation relating to the panel.

'And there's something else,' she said. 'I'd like it to be restored in time for my daughter's birthday. I forgot to mention that yesterday.'

'That's fine,' I automatically responded. It wasn't fine, I was fairly certain. I knew it was beyond my authority to be making such promises and yet the reassurances continued. 'We'll be able to work something out. It'll be fine.'

My own amenability startled me. After hanging up, I held on to the receiver and glared at the phone as though to urge the finished conversation to a different conclusion. I cursed myself and my infuriating tendency not to say what needs to be said at the moment that it is required. But I had never encountered anything so old—or so odd—during my employment as a conservator. My favourite commission up to that time had been a lurid 1980s acrylic painting that was rapidly discolouring due to its hairspray varnish. Usually, I was treating nineteenth-century landscapes with their relatively predictable problems and vistas. You sometimes joked about those pictures, asking cheeky questions about my progress on a patch of sheep fleece.

That's the only excuse I had for being so scatty. That I was overwhelmed by the object. Later, of course, I was overwhelmed more particularly with a love for the object, but that feeling was only beginning to seed.

When I turned around, Joy was watching. The lab at the Centre, which, incidentally, you never once visited, was devoid of privacy partitions. The ceiling was very high, the floor was very hard and the ensuing acoustics meant that every word anyone spoke bounced towards every other person in the space.

'What's the matter?' Joy asked me. 'You look a bit upset.'

You'd remember Joy; I whinged about her enough. Despite our shared title of Paintings Conservator, I was less experienced, a slight status distinction she rarely overlooked. She delighted in telling anecdotes that incorporated allusions to my later arrival at the workplace.

'Have you overcommitted?' she persisted.

'Maybe,' I answered, not bothering to bullshit.

'Oh well. You can always call the client back and set her straight. When I got that early Nolan, I was a bit excited too, made all sorts of stupid promises. Gillian forced me back on the phone the very next day. But it was all okay in the end. Remember?'

'No,' I sighed. 'That must have been before I worked here.'

'Of course, yes,' she laughed. 'That was before your time.'

'Would you like a cup of tea, Joy?' I asked her then, making my way to the door. I made inordinate numbers of hot drinks each day, usually to escape from my colleague. Giggle from Joy, Earl Grey; it was a well-developed reflexive behaviour.

I made the teas in the sanctuary of the kitchenette with its shelves full of BYO funny mugs and its countless banal, carefully laminated announcements. *Do not open dishwasher if cycle is on. Please rinse your own cup's and plate's. Tea coffee milk sugar and biscuits are for everyone.* (Never having worked in an office environment, you might not have encountered such things. Except maybe in a dressing room, near a stained cream sink and mirrors bordered by globes.) I added a dash of skinny milk and two little pellets of chemical sweetness to Joy's tea, stirring them swiftly inside the mug. *Joy to the world!* a faded angel trumpeted from the side of her white crockery. My own mug—adorned with a Barbara Kruger image from an exhibition we'd seen years before—appeared to be replying to the singing cherub nearby. *Don't Be a Jerk* it implored in a weighty dark font.

Gillian bounded into the room and threw an apple core in a perfect arc to the bin. 'So, how did the Poulos phone call go?' she asked.

'Okay. Not much info at all, really,' I said, dodging the problem of the time constraint I'd already imposed on the project.

'Maybe this is going to turn into a *thrilling* art mystery.' Gillian smiled. 'An *epic* saga all about proving that we've got ourselves an undiscovered masterpiece.'

'By some famous dead man?' I joined in.

'Yes, yes! And in the end, we'll realise this small work of art is worth millions of dollars and Mrs Poulos will be encouraged to donate it to a public institution for the cultural wellbeing of future generations.'

I rolled my eyes in mock horror.

Gillian turned and left the kitchenette as her laugh resonated through the building.

That afternoon, I was officially granted principal responsibility for the blue panel. Gillian called me into her office and told me that I'd been assigned the project. She looked at me closely, staring from behind her alarmingly pale eyelashes, and announced, 'It's all yours. You'll just be consulting with me about the key procedural decisions.'

I remained mute.

'I thought it would be a great project for you. Something different. A real *challenge*.' Gillian's earrings were swinging and I fixed on them—green triangles tapping gently against her freckled white neck. 'Well?' she insisted.

'Yes, thank you,' I managed. 'I love it. I'd love to.'

'Terrific.' She turned and left the room, neatly clipping the interaction.

She was professional, in the way that 'professional' can be a synonym for emotionally detached. In the time I'd worked with her, the closest thing I'd seen to a genuine outburst was when she'd excitedly clapped her hands after Joy had revealed a renowned, previously concealed signature on a painting. 'I knew it!' Gillian had applauded with her large amber rings clicking together. 'I knew it.' But that was an unusual situation, coming at a time when the Centre needed to justify a funding boost. She usually displayed a jaunty impassivity.

'They are not corpses,' Gillian had said to me in my job interview. 'They are cultural artefacts that can benefit from our skills. Remember that.'

Her catchcries about expert detachment were as contagious as her loud, head-thrown-back laugh, and those two person-ality traits combined to set the tone at my workplace. Gillian striding around the lab, Gillian gently teasing a conservator, Gillian being all feisty in meetings as she discussed her 'team'. Gillian, with her handcrafted asymmetrical attire held together by large brooches sourced from innumerable local artisans, was a woman who filled the spaces she moved through. Her bosom, her laugh, her voice textured by a long commitment to cigarettes, were all abundant and abundantly attractive. Even when I felt as prepared as possible—when I'd got my clothes right for the working day, when I'd found a combination of garments to reflect that quirky-serious-art-world look I always sought, when I was working with competence and care, even when my words emerged with a well-timed wit—I often felt insubstantial conversing with

Gillian. I felt like a girl pretending to be a grown-up, an employee pretending to be an authority.

When she gave me responsibility for the angel panel, I was struck by an unprecedented professional thrill. I'd previously followed her approach to the work, never becoming emotionally attached to a project. You could attest to that; I rarely went on about my paintings at home. But with the assignation of the blue picture, I felt as though I'd just received a commission to restore the Mona Lisa. I longed to build a partition around my workbench or install a laser alarm system so no one else could have access to it. I imagined leaping like a crazily protective parent between the painting and anyone who dared to touch it.

I stayed at work late that evening, again somewhat unprecedented. Joy found me reading articles in the research office as she left to go home.

'Still here?' she barked.

I swivelled around on the navy office chair. I'd been reading conference papers: *Nineteenth-Century Cradle Supports on Renaissance Panel Paintings: Issues in Removal—A Symposium.* The title was visible at the head of the document and I had a schoolgirlish urge to shield the words with my arm.

'You're not wasting any time getting on with it,' Joy said. 'You must be worried, though? Such an old picture.'

'I am a bit worried,' I obliged.

'Well, don't be,' she said with a furrowed brow, 'but if there is anything, *anything* at all I can do to help with the project, you must let me know.'

'Okay.'

And at that moment, just as Joy offered her collaborative services with a zealous charity, I felt a deep pang of possessiveness. It made me shift in the ergonomic chair, sitting up straight and breathing deeply. I had never felt anything like it, except perhaps with you in the early days. That pull. That sudden disappearance of choice.

Joy nodded and left with a final smile. I focused on reading the conference paper.

The work continued. I took photographs of the panel before any of the conservation procedures began: the front picture plane, the reverse with its cradle tugging at the wood, the flat edges sawn off and never sanded. I took photos of the woodworm damage, of the mottled flaking paint layers, of the knot in the poplar where a branch had once grown, until I amassed a whole folio of 'before' shots in preparation for the transformative makeover. The process enhanced my intimacy with the painting until I felt acquainted with its every millimetre.

One of the angels was composed of gentle tones with each kicking leg shaped by blended colour. Almost every pore of that cherub was a bristle brushstroke made with tiny hatches of paint. The other angel was more vigorous; its body was made with loosely broad sweeps of paint, piled in layers to create its form. Perhaps the artist was experimenting, practising and playing with method. Or maybe it was a careful choice to create two distinct individuals: two bodies flying in their own way through the same resplendent sky.

After the photographs, I examined the panel under raking light. When the lamp is positioned on the perfect oblique angle, so much more appears: grooves in a surface that had seemed paper smooth; minute cracks announcing an age that is otherwise disguised. Small lines in the painting's gesso primer appeared like the watermark on a banknote. The wipes of the artist's brush were visible across the length of the wood. Those strokes deviated slightly towards the edge of the panel as though the artist's arm was held awkwardly and unable to sustain the movement. I imagined a young apprentice leaning over, sweeping the brush and frowning. Sleeves rolled up, away from the paint.

Under the light, I could see the distribution of the blue more clearly. Applied after the angels, it tided around them, building up at the soft edges of their limbs and wings: small ridges of ultramarine like breaking waves against their curves. The knot in the wood—concentric ridges covered in sky— resembled a twisting weather pattern with its vapours fizzing together in the windy blue: a visible flaw and a touch of looming storm.

∾

During those days, I spoke to you several times. You diligently called me from each stop on your Four Play tour.

'What does the tour have to do with sex?' I'd asked you.

'Nothing,' you'd laughed. 'The foreplay reference just attracts attention. Eases people into the idea. Kids with surging hormones, you know.'

And so, you were off, one of four actors scooting around regional Victoria performing plays on the theme of 'getting started'. Cheesy motivational stories for young people, you'd said, about their growing independence, leaving home, finding a job, all the big issues.

When I spoke to you during those weeks, we discussed everything except what was preoccupying me at work. We talked about the Harrietville Motor Inn where you were staying: its agapanthus and its trampoline. We talked about your audiences, how there was invariably a teenager ejected from each show for sending text messages during the performance. We talked about the weather, how much we missed each other, mutual friends. But I never once mentioned the panel painting. Or the Rotting Room in our flat.

We were breaking up at this time, as you know. We had been breaking up for a year or so, I suppose, if I look honestly at what was happening between us. But there is a certain nobility in persistence, in working through a relationship. That idea sustained me for too long. I wanted to hold on and be *mature* and acknowledge that relationships need *work*. We'd been going on deliberate dates and making self-conscious attempts to *engage* with one another for months. Even after all that has happened, I can recognise the absurdity of that approach. Maybe after a decade of marriage or a couple of kids or even, to be completely practical, a bit of shared financial property, it might be appropriate to work on a commitment. But we were just stubbornly attached to our initial romanticism, our swift cohabitation, and the habit of our togetherness prevailed. There wasn't anything noble about it; if anything, it was evidence of a weakness and, perhaps, a gentle love that still pulsed between us. I needed the small barbs of hate to begin before I could be honest about our situation. That is something I regret.

During the days of your absence, I was entirely absorbed by work. The panel filled my thoughts—the tug of its apparently supportive cradle and the damage it was doing to the picture surface. Research had confirmed my initial suspicion: while removal of the nineteenth-century cradle was an extreme operation, it was essential to the stabilisation of the artwork. I'd emailed other conservators overseas, colleagues with more expertise on Renaissance panel paintings than anyone at the Centre. Reply after reply had arrived expressing a unanimous opinion: removal of the cradle was a 'necessary risk' or a 'precarious requirement' or a 'difficult obligation'.

The cradle was fighting with the curving wood and causing it to split, top and bottom, along the grain. The panel wanted to curl, the cradle wanted to stop it and that tension was causing the whole object to lose solidity. Removing a cradle is a violent action. Like suddenly letting go of a person you're holding on to, physics suggests that one of you will start to fall. The paint was gripping the panel and the panel was gripping the cradle and the material co-dependence would be hard to rebalance. Still, I knew that it was necessary. I knew that those two angels had to be released from the pull of past conservation and allowed to fly around their portion of twisting tree trunk like a pair of happy bugs.

These were the things I thought about. At home, in the evenings, I'd potter around, occasionally going into the Rotting Room, noting the mess, noting the still-wet floor, deciding not to deal with it, and closing the door once more.

I often looked at my mirror, surrounded by images, which hung on a wall in our bedroom. When we'd moved into the flat together, I'd been quite insistent about the mirror's method of transportation. I'd carried it in the car like a precious fishbowl, horizontally across my lap, refusing to extract the layers of historical detritus tucked into its frame. There was the Rothko reproduction torn from a magazine: a shape the colour of old blood floating in an orange juice wash. A Goya monster eating a bawling baby. Two cards that depicted artists performing in their own art: a photograph of Cindy Sherman staring into her camera, pretending to be a movie star, and an equine Matthew Barney in a moulded rubber mask. There was also a picture of the half-cleaned

Sistine Chapel that had inspired me when I'd first begun my art conservation study: a revelation of gelato-coloured figures floated in the clean section of ceiling while the grime of the untouched part suffocated the bodies beneath it.

You were there, of course, peering out with a painted red face from behind a couple of favoured birthday cards, in one of the photos I'd taken on the day we met. You'd been acting in a play; I had the job of photographing it and I'd been struck by your resonant voice and solid poise. And then, once I moved in for the close-up, I found your eyes. Those eyes that were already on me. I tripped on the steps in the theatre aisle. You smiled and finished the play. But, you know all this: how immediately we fell in love. And it seems so strange to remember the start of us. How infatuated and self-satisfied we were in our bubble. It descended so quickly—our small globe of happiness—and we were so sure and delighted in the certainty of what we'd found.

Sometimes, now, when I am wandering through strange streets and laneways, I see a young couple and recognise them. Their flushed faces and watery eyes, their fingers searching for a way to reach into skin through too many clothes when any clothes at all would be too many, their leaning, contented bodies. And, sometimes, I have an idiotic compulsion to warn them. Once, I even approached the most beautiful pair of lovers you could imagine. *Scusi*, I said. They looked up at me, almost dreamily with half-smiles and surprised brows, and I couldn't speak. *Be careful, cherish yourselves, don't be together, don't be apart, love, love, love.* But I couldn't speak. So I hurried away, adjusting my bag on my shoulder, like a confused tourist. Which, I suppose, is what I really was.

∾

One day when I arrived at work, Gillian confronted me when I'd barely had a chance to remove my coat.

'You've been neglecting the lofty hunters, haven't you?' she said.

She was referring to another painting I'd been assigned to restore, one I'd hardly touched since the blue panel's arrival. It was a provincial hunting scene painted in homage to a recently deceased farmer, featuring several dead and still-living family members in anachronistic hunting garb on a hill peak on their property. The old farmer had painted over the visage of his wayward brother a decade earlier and the new owner—the farmer's son—wanted the additional paint removed and his uncle's face restored to the scene.

Gillian smiled at me and waited.

'Yes,' I admitted. 'I think I might have to put it aside for a little while.'

'Go on,' she said.

'It's this,' I continued, nodding towards the angels. 'I need to focus on this.'

'Can't you handle a bit of multi-tasking, sweetie? What are you? A bloke?'

'No, no,' I said, absurdly.

'Well?'

'Well, I promised Ana Poulos that we could restore her panel in time for her daughter's birthday, in a couple of months. It's a family heirloom and she thinks that would be the right time to hand it on. And I know I shouldn't have promised anything, but I did. And I'm sorry and I do think it'll be possible if I just concentrate on that—'

'Okay, okay,' Gillian said to stop my rambling. 'If this is going to be your sole project for a while, we'll need more money from the client. It's as simple as that.'

I nodded as she turned away. 'Gillian?'

'Yes?'

'The cradle support needs to be removed.'

'Are you sure?' She lowered her chin and her voice to a serious pitch.

I nodded towards the emails I'd received, pinned to the corkboard above my bench. 'I've sought opinions from people in the UK, Italy.'

Gillian stared for a moment, then flung her hands up in the air, threw her head back and laughed. 'You get the money, you can do the work!'

On the other side of the lab, Joy dropped a cleaning swab, hurriedly picked it up off the floor and continued working with a wry, uncontained smile.

I sighed and turned around to face the angels.

❧

Two days later, it happened.

The wax resin paper held the paint with the most delicate touch. I rolled it out onto the workbench, placed the panel down onto it and they merged, the layers of colour settling softly into the mixture on the paper like a leaf into sand.

The cradle came off easily after that, lifting away with a small amount of chiselling, the old glue quite prepared to let go. The released panel almost seemed to sigh. I imagined that I could see the parts of it easing achingly back into place, like a person trying to crack a neck bone after too much exercise. The discarded cradle sat on the bench beside me, redundant, as I began to examine the bare back of the poplar plank. I brushed. The strings of dust. The nestled flakes of dirt. I held a gentle vacuum against the wood.

And then I saw it—a name on the back. Neat and large. *Caterina*. With a C.

Eight letters in clear black ink: *Caterina*.

2

VENICE, 1478

'...this morning I began to apply the azure, and it can't be
left; it's very hot, and the glue could go bad at any moment.
In another week I will have finished this level and I think
you will want to see it before I remove the scaffolding.'

BENOZZO GOZZOLI, LETTER TO PATRON, 1459

Imagine it for a moment. A man with a bad headache,
standing on the edge of a scaffold.

He has just put his right foot into a bucket of plaster
and can feel it hardening on the hairs of his calves. He yells
down at an apprentice who is crouching on the ground over
a dish of red pigment with his arms bending back like a
pair of chicken wings as he grinds the paste with a stone.
The boy is engrossed in the grind and the hardened-hair
man has to shout and shout.

'Niccolò, *ciao*, Niccolò,' he yells.

The boy looks up, gasping and gaping at the master above him.

'*Sì, maestro,*' he squeaks as he jumps to his feet, pulling at his crushed cream smock.

The master barks at the boy to refill the bucket of plaster. Quickly. The man watches the boy, his large flat hands reaching up the scaffold, grabbing a trowel, stirring the mixture, wiping his face. He returns the bucket. Quickly, quickly. Because when you are painting frescoes, it's all in the timing.

Since Giuseppe de Rossi was convicted of fraud in the Court of the *Arte dei Depentori*, all the other workshops in Venice have been in a permanent state of angst. Giuseppe substituted yellow tin for gold and cheap blue azurite for the rich ultramarine stipulated in his contract. He was commissioned to paint an altarpiece and several frescoes in the private chapel of a wealthy merchant on the cusp of death. The merchant sought a burial place teeming with spiritual grandeur painted in the most lavish materials available. But the merchant was dying and Giuseppe had to work fast. He hired extra assistants in order to complete the work before death descended: one to paint feet, another who was expert at delineating fabric folds. But Giuseppe was a greedy man and he resented the extra expense. He had, however, little cunning. His skimping was obvious and he was quickly arrested.

It became a grand scale scandal. Word of Giuseppe's fraud rushed through the canals of Venice like an effluent wave. It infected everyone, creating a heavy distrust between artists and patrons that caused people with usually open eyes to squint at each other and frown.

Niccolò, the young apprentice, is sad. His master, on the edge of a scaffold with a headache and encrusted plaster on his leg, has been acting strangely. He drops things and throws things and yells things at the wall when his paint patches dry in mismatched colours.

And it has been so hot. It isn't the stench that bothers Niccolò's master; it is the air. It's full and furry and causes the *giornata* to dry too soon. The paint leaks into the wet surface and becomes sealed as soon as the plaster dries. If the paint doesn't make it onto the wall in time, the whole section has to be scraped off and begun again. The stress of the process throbs in the master's temples and shovels at his brow from within. He compulsively bites his fingernails. He tears at the nails with his teeth, consuming *piccolo* portions of plaster and pigment. Maybe it is finally poisoning him, Niccolò thinks.

As the young apprentice looks up at his master and contemplates poisoning by pigment, he remembers that he has an errand to run. He grabs a small pouch from a table nearby, tucks it carefully into the pocket of his smock, and walks out of the heavy wooden town hall doors.

Niccolò moves along the narrow streets in the white glare of the afternoon. He sniffs occasionally and pulls at the downy hairs on his face.

Last night he had a dream. There was a woman in a bright blue Madonna robe staring at him as he dressed. She had waves of ebony curls and moist rosebud lips that kissed softly at the air around her. He'd woken up, sticky and ashamed, relaxing into his body.

He thinks about this as he walks with his big flappy feet pounding the slush. He crosses bridge after bridge, moving through the tenuous lagoon terrain. Some of the bridges are crudely slatted and he can see the swilling brown water beneath him. Niccolò tries not to clutch at his pocket, scared. But the water teases and gulps, inviting the pouch under his smock to fall like a pebble. *Plop.*

He is relieved to have left the town hall. His master is grumpy and clumsily old and Niccolò struggles to know how to help him. He longs to say something useful but instead he just prepares his materials. Sometimes, Niccolò watches his master progress through a segment of fresco and before any orders are given, the apprentice has the next piece poised for plastering. The master is always surprised by this and, once in a while, the frown on his face unfolds for a moment and he sighs. And that is enough for Niccolò.

Yesterday, the workshop received payment for a small commission completed several months ago—a fresco in the hall of the wine merchants' guild. The painting had been undertaken by several apprentices and for the first time since his entry into the workshop Niccolò was allocated responsibility for one part of the final image. The plump red grapes he'd painted onto the wall were so lovely that his master had quietly scolded him.

'Niccolò, the fruit is the most beautiful part of this,' he'd said with his dirty hand waving in front of the fresco. 'But a grape cannot be more than a man.'

'Forgive me, sir,' said the boy. 'Next time, you must also allow me to paint the people.'

At that, Niccolò's master had laughed at his young apprentice and turned away.

Yesterday morning, thirteen barrels of wine were deposited at the entrance to the workshop as final payment for the work. The apprentices were surprised at the arrival of the vessels and had sat on top of them, discussing their contents, wondering if a plaster trowel might serve to release their seal. The master emerged from his family lodgings moments after the wine delivery and, as was becoming increasingly typical, scolded the boys and ordered them to get on with the morning's preparations.

But today, Niccolò has an important errand. He walks on, crossing the market square, through swarms of people filling tattered woven baskets with food. He pushes past a crowded stand where the best prices are being sought for rosewater, eggs, almonds and ale. He slips on a caked dribble of shining yolk, clutches his pocket and tugs at his smock to compose himself. He winds his way through the hordes, catching a bunch of fennel as it tumbles from the top of a wooden crate, its flat musty planks providing a platform for display. The greengrocer shouts his thanks into the crowd but already Niccolò has passed.

It is a stifling day and the smells hang heavily over the boy; there is a sudden stench of briny sweetness as Niccolò passes a fishmonger stirring through a bucket of twitching salmon, their scales sparkling in the sun. He brushes a fluffy clump of hanging birds—pheasants, partridges and quails, ready to be released from their strings and roasted—as he manoeuvres through the square, skips over a rat and continues. Niccolò nods his regards to a large sweaty man selling sausage at the edge of the market. The man drops his bloody rag, waves eagerly at Niccolò and gestures towards his produce with a questioning face. The apprentice looks at the tangled tubes of rosy meat, shakes his head and smiles.

Niccolò walks on, focused on his destination. He is proud of his *maestro*'s trust, pleased at the secret he holds. The gold ducats in the pouch barely pull at his clothes but he can feel them, snug against his body, and safe.

The peeling brown shutters of the apothecary's shop have been pushed open and are bunched together on either side of the wide entrance. There is no barrier between the street and the building as Niccolò steps quickly inside.

He sees the apothecary, wipes his face and smiles, *buongiorno*.

He is here to collect five measures of the finest lapis lazuli stone that arrived in Venice two days earlier on an old barge from Afghanistan. The apothecary doesn't know the purpose of the visit, and would be giving Niccolò far more attention if he did. Instead, the young apprentice perches on a low stool in one corner of the room, watching portions of green clay and burnished gold coins exchange hands. *Terra verde*, thinks Niccolò, recognising the pigment. He looks around, waiting, while the hot wind from the street blusters through the open doorway.

The shop wall opposite Niccolò is covered in shelves on which stand cloudy glass vessels crammed with all manner of paints and potions. On the left side of the wall, the contents are medicinal—small curly objects that Niccolò has never seen before, phials of crystalline powders and bottles of thick syrupy tonic. On the right, the jars hold the painting materials he knows so well. There is one full of red sinoper pigment, crushed from the cinnabar stone, and a group of small containers stuffed with berries that will soon be pulverised into a useful crimson smear. There is a row of blue paints, stretching across half the width of the wall. There are two large flasks of dark fabric dye, made from the indigo plant. Next to those, Niccolò notes four jars of azurite powder. He thinks of the mine near Siena and how the workmen there are said to have hands that are permanently gloved in colour. The pigment he needs, however, is far too precious to be displayed in full view like the others.

Niccolò pulls the cloth pouch out of his smock pocket and begins to play with it like a carnival juggler. Right hand. Left hand. Right hand. Up. Down. *Wooooooo*. The ducats inside click happily together and Niccolò smiles to himself.

After several minutes of waiting on the stool, Niccolò is greeted by the apothecary who guides him into the far corner of the shop to begin their transaction. The apprentice tells the man what he requires and a quick silence falls between them.

'Ah, *sì, sì, sì,*' the apothecary says then, scurrying off to collect the treasure like a hunched and startled mole.

The man returns a moment later with five blue stones, opaque and lumpy, balancing on a tray.

The next day Niccolò's master is at home. The apprentices are alone at the town hall, painting and chattering to each other with more abandon than is usual. After a brief plaster fight and a scaffold-slipping incident in which the foot of the youngest boy was wedged under a hinge until he started to cry, they are now working. Their eager noses almost touch the wall as they lean in to the painting, filling in details with the finest red sable brushes.

There is a pouch full of lapis lazuli, waiting in a corner of the room.

Niccolò's master trusts his boys enough to refuse to get out of bed for this one day. His wife, Isabella, tiptoes through the house. She cooked him turnip soup that he refused to eat. She completed some accounts paperwork that he refused to sign. She asked him pleasant questions that he refused to answer.

'No disturbances today,' he finally shouted. 'Please, I want nothing.'

So, in accordance with his demand for silence and solitude, Isabella shooed their boisterous twins outside. Giorgio and Segna are four years old and like to yell; Isabella will spend most of her day keeping her growing sons from their aging father.

Later on, she is seen running through the streets of Venice holding a large bundle of cherries. Two matching, squealing little boys are chasing her. She starts to throw the cherries at her children, who respond as children do, by grabbing the closest thing and hurling it back. Unfortunately for Isabella, the closest thing is a dead white mouse. It hits her left ear with a muted thud and ricochets down her cleavage. Isabella stops, looks at her sons and slowly plucks the creature from between her breasts. Giorgio and Segna stand very stiffly, staring at their mother. Isabella holds the mouse at the end of its ridgy grey tail and swings it back and forth in front of her sons' eyes. When they are slightly hypnotised, she splashes the mouse into the nearest canal and scoops up the boys. One under each arm, she carries their exhausted bodies home, towards the nerves of their father.

When they arrive, Caterina has returned. The first and only daughter of the master left early this morning to visit the markets and now she is talking to her father about some fabric she saw at a stall.

'And down each strip was the most incredible crimson thread. Imagine, Papa, little stitches of it, like tiny drops of blood, all along the edge.' As she talks, Caterina grabs at the heavy cotton of her dress, fanning the hem with her small busy fingers. Her knees are bouncing up and down as she balances on a corner of the bed.

For a moment, Isabella, Segna and Giorgio stand at the doorway to the room, watching the pair. Isabella is forever watching this child.

Caterina's mother died in childbirth and her father married Isabella six years later. She inherited the little girl like she was a wealth of gems. She wanted to wrap her in velvet and hide her away forever, so huge was Isabella's recognition of the treasure of her. Instead, she proudly and protectively set about showing her new child to the world. And the world to the child. From the beginning, when the six-year-old had first embraced her new mother with a desperation that both scared and thrilled her, Isabella was captivated by Caterina. The way she sparkled despite her loss; the way she looked at things constantly, like there was always something particular to be found; her bright, frustrated beauty.

The twins worship their sister. They are singsonging for her now and interrupting this ponderous moment.

'Signorina Caterina. Signorina Caterina,' they call her.

Caterina stands up, runs towards the boys and tickles them.

'Do you have to be so noisy?' shouts the master, as he props himself higher in his bed.

The children leave the bedroom in a row, single file— dark heads lowered, trying to be good.

Isabella walks towards her husband, sits down beside him and takes his hand. She kisses it and places it slowly back onto the blanket. She strokes his fingers.

'Your hands,' she says to him. 'They are precious.'

'Oh, Isabella,' he says.

And his wife watches him clench the covers on either side of his legs. And she watches his fists—white and hard— as a tiny flake of pigment falls onto the bed.

Caterina likes to visit her papa in his workshop or, if he is managing a commission somewhere else, she will often travel to the other side of Venice.

Today, she walked for almost an hour to find him. As usual, she made sure that her journey led her past the San Zaccaria convent to the east of the city. She loves the nuns there, loves the focus of their small, proud faces.

Caterina passes by San Zaccaria every week and, each time, she stands behind one of the stone pillars at the entrance gate and looks through the small gaps in the wall at the women gliding across the convent's forecourt. The nuns live at the rear of the building, a fair distance away from the loud construction taking place at the façade. Caterina likes to watch the nuns passing by the stonemasons on the way to their lodgings; they appear so undisturbed by the noise, just accepting the workmen as part of the familiar San Zaccaria landscape. It's wonderful, she thinks, the way that the nuns continue on with their business while their world is reconstructed around them.

Caterina imagines the nuns decorating religious manuscripts in poorly lit rooms; she sees them painting page borders and intricate patterns on a single large letter until their eyes are hurting with the strain of detail. She imagines them worshipping in the existing chapel with its famous frescoes of floating saints, commissioning artists to embellish the newest white walls of the convent and enjoying banquets with the most enlightened members of the Venetian nobility.

After spying on the nuns today, Caterina continues the walk to her father. She arrives, stands one step inside the town hall and scans the bustle for her own place, trying to find a job for herself amid the frenzy of apprentices. She walks towards the side wall, seizes a broom that is almost twice her height and begins to sweep. Around the handle, her fingers are spread red with the effort of it.

Her father is gilding a halo. Standing on a rickety three-step ladder, he peels the pressed gold onto the wall too quickly. He scratches it and shouts. Steps off the ladder. Hits the wall with his fist. No one in the town hall turns towards his exclamation. Instead, all the bodies in the room move closer to what they are doing—in unison, they know not to notice.

Three apprentices are standing on a scaffold landing, close to the ceiling. One is reaching into the cornice with a brush soaked in paint and leaving the tiniest white dabs. Another leans towards a thin tin bucket, glances inside, stirs. Niccolò is filling in the sky with a broad fur brush. He is distracted because of the *maestro*'s daughter, sweeping the floor and humming. She is hardly making any sound but Niccolò still strains to hear her tune. He can hear the high hums best but only when her broom bristles aren't catching on something large and louder. He likes the way he has to concentrate to hear her; it makes him feel as though it is only him who has noticed that she is even humming at all.

Caterina has been visiting the workshop for years, yet it is only recently that the apprentice has become so aware of her; like a tree that you have walked past every day that is suddenly covered in blossom, and it is only then that you notice its beauty. Niccolò often tries to recall the child who he knows used to wander beneath the scaffolds when he arrived at the workshop, but he cannot grasp her image. To him, there is only this thirteen-year-old person with huge eyes that dart and stare. Sometimes even at him. And he is not really sure whether it is Caterina or himself who has changed.

Niccolò paints his sky with blue azurite, a notoriously fugitive pigment. He does not know, as he carefully works around wings and noble noses, that one day the sky will flake away and leave only patchy clouds of red underpaint, pushing through like a storm.

There is a pouch full of lapis lazuli, waiting in a corner of the room.

When the rest of the hall is completed the master will apply the pigment to the virgin's gown, to the governmental coat of arms, to the spaces where the wealth of the image is unquestioned. As stipulated in the contract.

Caterina frowns at the floor. There are chunks of plaster, shreds of rags, dust and paint peels, all catching in the bending broom bristles. She thinks about the boys around her—the same age as her and wearing smocks wiped with colour—and she doesn't understand why it is that she should only sweep.

Later, she will travel to a church beyond the canal web, sit in a pew and copy angels into the notebook she carries with her like her soul. She will look beyond the saints and the disciples glowing at the centre of the church's altarpiece and will peer instead at the chubby *putti* in the corners. With red chalk and charcoal dust, Caterina will shape her own wings and cherub cheeks until the smudges on her hands become bigger than the smudges on the page. Then she will close her book of drawings and leave.

She might pray for forgiveness on her way out. For the theft of the charcoal, of course.

❧

When Niccolò was eight years old, he told his father that he wanted to learn to paint. Then he enacted a paintbrush mime, making sweeping strokes through the air with a precocious flourish. His arms whipped about with so much vigour that his father could not ignore him.

Painting was a respectable trade. He would endeavour to find his son a position in a workshop by the eve of his eleventh birthday. The following year, Niccolò's aunt married an artist's brother and the requisite family connection was established. After years of distracted lessons, the partially educated Niccolò entered the *maestro*'s workshop with a fresh new smock and a tremendous yearning.

It was at about that time that Caterina began to draw angels. She favoured twins with ruddy faces and soft legs that folded in the air as they flew.

❧

The artists are working on a large fresco on the town hall's exterior wall. It's a warning to all Venetians to behave, with an image of a wrongdoer being banished from the city. There is some forked lightning sketched onto the sky and a haggard government official pointing the criminal towards oblivion across a wide and angry canal.

Caterina sits opposite the town hall, watching, and she thinks that the fresco is funny. It's the bronze horses on the San Marco Basilica that amuse her most. They have been painted leering at the banished man with their nostrils flaring, as though even sculptures have the capacity to be judgmental. It seems almost as if they might break away from their stands and gallop over the disgraced citizen as punishment. That should deter the criminals, Caterina thinks.

The details of the exterior fresco are outlined in the contract. *Stamp*. So is the input of Caterina's father; certain figures must be executed in 'the master's own hand' and the rest may be done by the apprentices. *Stamp*. Expected date of completion is also noted. *Stamp*. And there is the important materials clause, stipulating how much gold leaf can be used. *Stamp*. And how much lapis lazuli. *Stamp*. Sometimes Caterina thinks that her father looks trampled by all these guidelines.

The master is carrying a bucket of green paint, six paintbrushes, a palette knife, a design drawing and a box of charcoal. He drops two of the brushes and they splatter into a dirty brown puddle at his feet.

'Aah,' he shouts.

Several apprentices are there but it is only Niccolò who moves to assist his *maestro*. Niccolò retrieves the fallen brushes and carries them inside. Caterina sees this, as she sees most things, and decides she would like to talk to that boy. That boy who is kind to her father.

～

A week later, Caterina tells Niccolò three secrets. They are sitting in a small *piazza*, soaked in sunlight.

'I want to paint,' she says, 'but Papa won't allow it.'

Niccolò stares at her face, open and white, and he feels he might start to cry. 'I'm sorry,' he says after a long silence, his hand shading his eyes to look more closely at the girl.

'Well, Niccolò, I do my own work sometimes.'

'What do you mean?'

'I draw. In a notebook. And I have a small poplar panel. I took it from Papa's workshop and I am going to paint it. I know what to do. I've watched for so long. I know how to prepare the wood and mix the pigments.'

'Do you have the materials?' Niccolò asks.

'Well, some things. I take them.'

That was the second secret. Niccolò keeps watching her, waiting.

'There are places in Bologna where girls can be taught to paint,' she goes on. 'Did you know that?'

'No.'

'Well, there are. And perhaps one day I will go there because I know Isabella would understand and Papa is getting old.'

'So he might die soon?'

'Yes,' says Caterina.

And that was the third secret. That the master's loving daughter sometimes imagined his death as an amazing promise, as if it would release her into the only place she already knew.

∽

It is the end of the day and the setting ball of sun is pouring through new stained-glass windows. Niccolò, speckled in colour, is cleaning the town hall floor and thinking of Caterina. He feels a warmth for her that makes him still: a heavy, incredulous affection. Never before has he been so preoccupied by the presence of another person. His capacity to function has changed. He is moving differently. He is seeing differently. It is almost as though his whole world has been brushed with a gentle Caterina varnish that spreads and soaks into everything. Where he once saw his *maestro* as his *maestro*, now the man has become Caterina's papa, the person who will not let her paint. The *piazza* he crosses each day has become a place where Caterina sometimes sits. The floor he is now clearing is the one she has swept.

Niccolò moves across the town hall, picking up tools and piling them, one by one, against the wall. He reaches the far corner of the room. It is here that the unused pigments are waiting. He sees the pouch of lapis lazuli and Caterina plunges through his thoughts. Her angels, made without colour, wave their wings.

Niccolò picks up the pouch, undoes the brown drawstring and reaches inside to feel the five stones clicking together. His hand grasps one and he lifts it, like a small coin, out of the bag. He releases it into his pocket and the lapis lazuli rests alone against his body.

Later, he will grind and prepare the stone, sweeping the precious pigment dust into a small glass phial. Then he will give it to his friend.

∿

Caterina is in a room on the middle floor of their home. Beneath her, she can hear the scrapings of the workshop, the rush and the slush in the street, and her father shouting at an apprentice. Above her is the pressure of footsteps. Isabella, Segna and Giorgio are on the top floor, and from the way the ceiling beams are shaking, Caterina thinks that the twins must be having a jumping competition. They like to do that: stand side by side, count to three and try to fly straight up into the air. Isabella is infinitely patient with the game and she is often found adjudicating the boys' performance from the comfort of a nearby stool.

Moments ago, the twins wanted Caterina to play with them. They had been pulling on her, one arm each, and begging her to go outside. She had stared at them, taking in the eager love on their faces, and had not known what to say, how to explain that there was a half-finished painting hidden in a room of their home that she wanted to touch again.

'Giorgio and Segna, let your sister go,' Isabella had said. 'Caterina has things she wants to do.'

Caterina glanced at Isabella and smiled with gratitude.

Now, she looks at the image on the small poplar panel. She is very pleased with these angels, and their wings, especially. Each one is comprised of rows of feathers, from the curly down at the shoulder, through dense layers of white that become the long, almost translucent, quills at the edge. Sometimes Caterina spends hours sketching a pair of wings with precision. She goes over and over the sweep of their span until the plumes are perfect for flight. Without the right wings, she is worried that the cherubs might fall from the page. But the angels in front of her now are flying so well that they look as though they might just escape from the picture. They are floating, fat and free. Only the space where they are flying needs to be filled.

Caterina reaches for the phial of ground blue stone, empties it into a dish and mixes it with egg yolk in the careful way she has watched so often. The particles of pigment merge with the yolk until the threads of sticky colour evolve into a beautiful paint—opaque, like liquid enamel, the colour of a wide summer sky. For a moment, she thinks of Niccolò, smiles and whispers a *grazie* into the dish.

She paints around her twin angels with a multitude of lines. Like a pour of raindrops, the strokes bounce off the figures and slide into their rightful place. Soon the picture is complete. She considers adding some clouds but decides that she wants only the purity of blue. She loves the surface of it, the smooth, vapoury lightness of its air.

The ultramarine paint slowly hardens. Caterina wants to touch it and dig her fingers into its sheen. Instead, she leans forward and sniffs the colour, deeply inhaling its aroma. When it is safe to touch, she turns the panel over and dips a brush into some black Indian ink until the thirsty bristles are drenched with it. She writes her name on the bottom. Neat and large, with a curly C. Caterina.

She lets it dry for a moment and places it behind the *cassone*, the wooden chest in a corner of the room, where it rests snug against the wall like a shadow.

Each month, the officials of the *Arte dei Depentori* visit the workshops of the guild's members. At each inspection, the *maestro* is obliged to report to the officer any unusual dealings—late payments or dissatisfied patrons or delayed productivity—that might have occurred in preceding weeks. The visits are usually brisk. The official arrives, greets the workers and is taken to a quiet area of the shop. There, the *maestro* assures his comrade that business practice is going well, that the commissions are proceeding at the expected pace and that, indeed, there have been no irregular events.

Today, the *Arte dei Depentori* official is due to arrive at the workshop of Niccolò's *maestro*. It is early and the master's family is gathered around the breakfast table in their home above the shop. Isabella is seated at one end. Giorgio and Segna have finally settled, side by side, on two sturdy stools. Their legs swing above the floorboards as they spoon through the bowls of oats that Caterina has just put down in front of them. Isabella watches her husband at the other end of the table. Instead of eating, he gazes down at his food and Isabella can see the press of his jaw beneath his sparsely bearded skin. She wants to reach towards him, wants to hold his face in her hands and kiss it. But there are three children between them now and she smiles her family breakfast smile.

Caterina has just sat down on a bench opposite the boys. She scoops the oats into her mouth with neat efficiency, her spoon clicking the bottom of the ceramic bowl long before everyone else's food has been consumed. She looks up—at Isabella, at her father, at the twins opposite her. Beneath the table, Caterina lifts her bare feet off the floorboards and places her right foot on Giorgio's lap and her left foot on Segna's. There is a sudden yelp from both the boys as Caterina's bold cold toes land on their legs. She laughs as two grubby pairs of hands grab on to her ankles.

'Quiet!' growls their father.

'Don't be silly,' adds Isabella. And there is a small thud-thud as Caterina drops her feet back onto the floor.

'Have you finished?' Isabella asks the twins.

They quickly nod. Segna slides his bowl away from him to emphasise the point. Giorgio sits very still with his lips pressed closed and his fingers grabbing the edge of the table.

'Caterina, can you play with them for a while?'

'Of course, Mama.' And, at that, the children jump up and hurry from the room like school students suddenly released by the bell.

The adults remain at either end of the breakfast table, holding their spoons and looking at one another. Isabella eventually moves to Giorgio's vacated stool and waits for her husband to speak.

'The guild official will be coming today,' the *maestro* says.

'And that is concerning you?'

'Yes.'

'Why? You said that the commissions were going well, that your greatest problem was too much work.'

'Yes. But there is something I am obliged to report,' he says. 'A theft.'

'What happened?' Isabella asks, her arms reaching across the table and their faces whisker-close.

'Something went missing from the town hall and I believe one of the apprentices is responsible.'

'What was stolen?' asks Isabella.

'Some lapis lazuli.'

'Oh.'

'Yes. And the boy—'

'Yes?'

'—well, I think it was Niccolò.'

∽

A week later, the city of Venice is in tumult. The *Magistrato alle Acque*, the man responsible for managing the flow of the canal waters, has recognised a pending flood. The populace is at work placing bulky sandbags at the doorways of buildings and praying to God that the roar of water will be contained. Rising floods are a common enough problem in their city and the mechanisms of protection are well established. The citizens know what to do, where to move their possessions and where to erect the heavy barriers of sand.

Despite the flood preparations, the court of first instance is in session and committed to the proceedings of the day. There are many cases to be heard, including a dispute over an artist's will. His drawings, pattern books and all other implements of the profession have been left to an artless relative; family members who worked within the man's workshop are appalled. There is a petition for clemency from a banished rapist and a dispute between a glassblower and his landlord over the inflated rent for a furnace. But the first case to be heard is that of Niccolò de Marco's charge of theft.

The head magistrate straightens his hat, strokes his long, wispy beard and begins to speak.

'Dishonour to the guild is dishonour to the state of Venice . . . The confession to the crime does little to alleviate its seriousness. In claiming responsibility, while refusing to explain the motivations for his behaviour, Niccolò de Marco has shown himself to be a stubborn and uncooperative servant of the Lord. As a citizen of this state, Niccolò de Marco has committed two crimes. Firstly, the theft of the lapis lazuli—a highly valued commodity amongst merchants and artists alike. Secondly, his commitment to silence that has served only to delay the proceedings in our otherwise expeditious court.

'After consultation with the officials of the *Arte dei Depentori*, the magistrates of the court have resolved to remove the thief from his position as apprentice in a workshop of the guild. His membership of the *Arte dei Depentori* is annulled. Accordingly, from the next Monday of this month, Niccolò de Marco is forbidden to enter the guild buildings or participate in any aspect of its activities.

'The magistrates have agreed that the boy's lack of cooperation and disregard for the proceedings of the court warrant an additional punishment. From the next Monday of this month, Niccolò de Marco is forbidden in any area north of the Grand Canal, including the bridge Rialto. He has shown himself to have an incomplete notion of the responsibilities of Venetian citizenship and is undeserving of complete access to the Venetian state.'

The mallet bangs on the court bench. Niccolò jumps in his chair.

And at this moment, just as Niccolò is banished and his *maestro* is trying not to weep in a corner of the courtroom, the canal waters are continuing to creep up the walls of the city. Drip by drip, puddle by puddle, a flood is starting to form.

❧

Niccolò stands together with the *maestro* in the large studio workshop. He has come to say goodbye to the old man whose trust he has betrayed. The *maestro* leans on a workbench, his palms stretched out around the materials on top, his thumb resting on the edge of a bowl of red vermilion pigment. His other hand presses down into some drawings and a small accounts book with a tired, torn spine.

Niccolò knows that this will be the last time he stands in this workshop, talks to his master, breathes on these supplies. He watches the red pigment shaking in the bowl as his hands twist inside the deep pull of his pockets.

'Did you sell the stone to another workshop?' the *maestro* asks.

'No.'

'Did you sell it to someone else?'

'No.'

'Have you kept it for yourself for some reason?'

'No.'

'Did you give it away?'

'No.'

'Are you going to tell me why you took the lapis lazuli?'

'No, I'm not. I'm sorry.'

Niccolò feels sick, but his conviction is consistent. His answers float out into the air—of the *Arte dei Depentori* rooms, of the court and, now, of the workshop—becoming solid and important before he has the chance to catch them. No. No. No. No, Niccolò hears himself saying, just the sound of the words making him stand up straight. Somehow, his love—he supposes that's what it must be—has nestled into him and made him speak this way.

'You are a stubborn boy,' the *maestro* says. 'And I will miss you.'

'*Grazie.*'

'What will you do, Niccolò?'

The boy looks up from the shaking red pigment and fixes on the eyes of the *maestro* for the first time. He has seen this man in so many moods. All those expressions that are wiped across his face with an alarming visibility: the harried, gasping face of the artist unable to accept his own increasing clumsiness; the scolding man snapping harsh words from his sneering mouth; the headache face—blinking eyes, a page of lines on his forehead and a neck that cannot move; the liquid gentleness of his expression whenever he is conversing with Isabella. Niccolò has always favoured that last one and he has often been busy in the workshop, praying that the *maestro*'s wife would come downstairs and talk to the old man so the apprentices could watch his grumpiness retreat. But this expression now—this version of the old man's face—Niccolò has never seen. He looks wounded. Almost childlike. He resembles a confused boy who has been deemed too young to hear a secret. Niccolò feels so much shame at the sight of this that his eyes fall back to the pigment bowl once more.

'I am planning to seek a job with an apothecary, sir,' the boy announces to the workbench. 'On the *terraferma.*'

'You're leaving?'

'Yes. As you heard, I am no longer allowed in this region of Venice. I would rather live beyond the city than stay here with the Grand Canal as my boundary.'

'Yes,' says the old man. 'An apothecary?'

'I think it could be a way of using my knowledge. If I can find a shopkeeper who will have me.'

'Perhaps you can specialise in Afghan trades, Niccolò: emeralds, copper, lap-is la-zu-li.'

The boy looks up at the *maestro* to check his face for any indication of a joke. Yes, a cheeky twinkle has found some room in the artist's wounded eyes. Niccolò smiles at the man. 'Perhaps,' he says.

And the mood is broken now by a noise at the entrance of the workshop. The two of them spin around towards the clatter of a falling tin bucket.

Caterina, stunned-faced and pale, turns and runs away. Her heavy brown dress bunches up around her legs as she disappears down the street.

3

The dream started with a thick green wave as I stood in a sort of city. The wave rushed towards me before I could move, so quickly that I could only watch it descend over me like a net, drenching my head, then my chest, then my whole body until my clothes were flatly heavy with the water and I was away. It carried me completely and, for a moment, there was only green—surging, twisting green— and muffled noises of smashing and grating screams. I hit a rooftop with a thud and was draped over it like a ragged piece of flotsam. I spluttered onto the sloping slime-covered tiles as the wave continued. All that remained from its path was a blank squelchy landscape with deep pools of water in places. It stretched interminably, eliminating the distinction between land and sea.

It was very quiet and it seemed that all life had been eradicated. But then, as I began to slide from the roof, I saw a movement and I knew that someone else had survived: a whole family. They were moving within the slush, breathing in and out decisively, and they didn't seem bothered by the water in their nostrils that rushed inside and gushed through their lungs. They just kept on wading through it all with easy amphibious transitions. And I knew their names. I recognised them. Coral and Ray were Mum and Dad. Three kids—Finn, Gil and Marina, and Granny, Pearl. I watched as Marina got hassled by her brothers. She was a hefty child, a solid presence in the water. Gil and Finn were small and twitching, constantly flipping through the sludge with sudden darting manoeuvres. Pearl was a white-haired lady with glowing translucent skin and a fetching pink dress that clung, saturated, to her curves. Ray had slick hair, sharp features and a sneaky edge. Coral was the character, though: all froth and colour and unexpected revelations. She appeared so soft but I noticed the spiky nails on her digits that would cut through anything that got too close.

The family couldn't see me. They moved past as I struggled to hold on, spitting out the green and shivering. And as I watched these cool, adaptable beings, the wave returned and I thrashed about, trying to breathe, pulling at the bedsheets as they tangled around me like sinewy grasping weeds.

Several times I woke up in the darkness, terrified. I'd wander to the kitchen and turn on the tap for a drink of clean water.

Later, of course, I thought again of that recurring dream. The desperate surge. The clinging. The eventual letting go.

～

My work continued, not without its difficulties. There is a particular encounter that I want to explain to you; it occurred on the day of your return from the tour.

Gillian and I were standing together with the panel lying in front of us—a vulnerable, passive specimen. I'd recently learnt that Ana Poulos was unable to afford the extra cost required to have the panel completed within the time constraints I'd accepted.

'I'll work nights, weekends, in my own time. And I'll explain any delays to the other clients, to the lofty hunters,' I pleaded.

'What will you say?' Gillian asked. 'That you've got a better offer?'

'No, no. I'll just tell them that we're waiting for a particular solvent or pigment, something plausible. It'll be fine.'

'Anyway,' Gillian said, glancing at the angels. 'I hope she realises that this picture won't ever look pristine. It's almost beyond repair.'

I saw the five centuries of nestled dirt, the paint that could float away in the wrong breeze, the warping panel with its hungry woodworm burrows. And I imagined Caterina and her patiently painted twins, still flying across the aching, aging wood; their wings a gentle flag, quivering. And I thought of her name on the back.

'It didn't even start with a great chance of survival—the way the materials were applied,' Gillian continued.

But I was insistent. I told her I would not accept that the panel could be allowed to further deteriorate because the person who made it might not have understood the ideal way to manipulate her materials. Because she didn't have enough time or varnish or paint products to hold her image secure. Because she might have learnt in fragments, grabbing on to whatever she could. From a distance.

'Okay, okay. Do you really want to be spending all your time in here? You've—'

'Yes.'

'—you've never been one to work after hours.'

'I know,' I accepted. 'But this is different.'

'And Mark?' she asked then, surprising me.

'He'll cope,' I replied, dogmatic.

It hadn't occurred to me to consider you in those plans. I admit that now.

'You're very sure about this, aren't you?'

'I am.'

'Alright. I've never seen you so obsessed. I can't argue with it. But be careful,' she warned. 'We can't fix everything, you know. Sometimes there *is* too much damage.'

'There's a signature,' I announced, trumping Gillian.

She folded her arms over her bosom and waited. I pulled on a pair of white gloves and lifted up the fragile painting, turning it over to reveal the name.

'Caterina,' she read. 'Caterina with a C. Oh dear.'

We leant towards it, watching the word with great intensity as though afraid to miss an unanticipated movement of its letters. 'Caterina' remained still, of course. Still, and defiantly legible across the poplar.

'Should I research this?' I asked. 'Should I find out about this before I do anything else?'

'Well, you don't have time, do you?' Gillian said with dismissive pragmatism. 'You'll just need to get on with the procedures.'

And she left me alone, staring at that name on the reverse of the picture.

I want you to see. To see how important the painting was becoming to me. How I was changing in ways that I was not then able to explain.

∾

Later that day, I was sitting at my workbench, surrounded by the panel's documentation. All its layers had been pulled apart and classified by light-filled machinery. Pages of paper, covered in numbers and graphs, recorded the pigments on the surface: copious genuine ultramarine and fragments of its synthetic replica, traces of rosy colour modelling the angels' form.

I held an x-ray up to the window and looked again at all that it revealed: splotches of lead white paint on the cherubic curves, the circle of knotted wood, the shadow of the discarded cradle and the delicate lines of woodworm burrow like cotton threaded through. I could see the grain of the poplar crossing beneath some planing grooves. They latticed together in miniscule grid lines, imperfect and crooked.

A composite image of the charcoal underdrawing flashed on the computer screen nearby. Countless reflections of infrared had identified the carbon-based materials hidden beneath the paint layers—those preparatory lines that had previously sneaked into sight only in the most transparent sections. The image on the monitor resembled a paused foetal ultrasound: smudges of colourless bodies together in a viscous cushion, the rounded flesh of two promised babies. On screen, the wings were rendered with a skeleton clarity— the precisely executed plan for her painting. They were the most meticulously drawn part of Caterina's picture and so much neater than the cherubic flesh and faces. When the underdrawing on the panel was first revealed, the perfection of those wings was astonishing. I thought of the Renaissance painters who were employed for the details—a foot specialist, an expert at architectural rendering—and I understood: wings were Caterina's thing. She fixated on the wings. And I could imagine so many reasons why.

'Your little ray of sunshine is home tonight,' Gillian said, suddenly behind me.

'Yes, he's back.' I was due to meet your minibus at Spencer Street Station at the end of the Four Play tour.

'Is he prepared for the new you?'

'What do you mean?' I asked, genuinely perplexed.

'Does he know about the panel painting?'

'No, not yet.' I started to straighten some items on my bench, preparing to leave.

'Oh well,' said Gillian. 'You'll have a lot to talk about then.'

Looking back, it appalls me that what was so obvious to my boss had escaped my attention. That what happened afterwards was the extreme event I needed to recognise it.

I pulled up at the kerb just as you all started to get out of the minibus. You didn't see the car immediately so I waited inside it for a moment, watching you and, I admit, savouring the view. I never tired of your face, nor had it neutralised through all our years of familiarity. There were times that I would glance at you and again be genuinely moved by your beauty. It was a helpful phenomenon.

You were struggling with that huge old suitcase you insisted on taking wherever you travelled. (It was with you then; it might still be with you now.) A functional backpack or even a modern bag with wheels would never suffice; it had to be your grandpa's suitcase with its brown cardboard sides, dirty metal corners and streaks of leftover labels. 'It reeks of the romance of travel,' you'd often said to me. It certainly reeked of something.

Your other particular travel habit was an insistence on sending postcards. For each town you visited, a card would arrive in our letterbox: usually an anti-scenic postcard—the daggiest, cheapest looking card available. You'd sent me one from Bright; it was the last such card I would ever receive. It featured a row of old workers' cottages with some spindly bushes lining the gutter. It was a grey, listless day and most of the postcard was consumed by a grey, listless sky. A poster supporting the local footy team was visible inside one of the front windows. On the back, in frail type, were the words *Colonial Cottages, Historic Highway*. It reminded me of the muted pictures I'd taken on primary school camp when we'd been given fifteen minutes to wander around a town without supervision and were so thrilled by the freedom that the whole place seemed worthy of photographic record. You thought those postcards were so funny, ironic. I usually agreed with you, although occasionally I just thought they were ugly; that last one from Bright was thrown into the rubbish bin far too soon.

You dropped your suitcase onto the footpath and sighed. You looked as though you'd been napping for most of the journey; there were creases on your face, perhaps from a scrunched-up jacket pillow pushing into your skin. I moved behind the minibus, past its obligatory stripe of stickers, before jumping out in front of you.

You yelped and opened your arms.

When we got into the car, you immediately noticed the old blue beads on my wrist.

'That new?' you said.

So I began to explain: the meeting with Ana Poulos, her panel, my responsibility. I had taken some photos from work, which I said I'd show you when we got home. You never asked to see them and I just took them back to the Centre the following day.

When we walked inside our flat, it was as though my time was up, as though a silent buzzer had gone off to indicate that it was your turn to talk. I didn't insist; I didn't try to assert the significance of it all. You assumed that because you had been the absent person, you were the one with the stories, that home was just the same, in that unimaginative way we all like to assume home will be after a journey. So I listened to you tell me about the Four Play tour. It had been more interesting than some of the previous trips, with perkier kids and better performance spaces and a more cohesive group of actors. You told me how positively the plays had been received, how the audiences responded well to your characters and how the director had a new production in the pipeline.

'It's a reworking of *Waiting for Godot*,' you explained. 'And I'm going to be playing Pozzo. We've got La Mama for a two week season.'

I'm sure I responded with the right sort of supportive enthusiasm.

'The rehearsals are starting straightaway,' you said. 'Sorry.'

'Sorry?'

'Well, they're all going to be in the evenings. Couple of the cast have day jobs.'

'That's okay.'

'Is it?' You were surprised. 'I thought you might claim spousal neglect.'

'No, no, it'll be okay,' I laughed. 'I'm going to be working late pretty much every night for a while.'

'You poor thing,' you said. I remember that exactly.

'No, I'm actually looking forward to it,' I corrected. And I was about to begin my second attempt to explain the panel when you suddenly stood up.

'There's a weird smell in here,' you announced. 'Like mould or damp?'

I tried to reach your arm and pull you back down to the couch. 'Don't worry, it's—'

'It certainly doesn't smell normal.'

'—okay. It's nothing.'

But you were off. 'Is it coming from the study?' you insisted, walking towards the odour, your twitching nose leading the way like a rabbit. You opened the door on the Rotting Room and went inside.

'Fuck,' you yelled. 'There's some kind of flood in here!' A typically theatrical exaggeration.

I followed you into the room.

4

VENICE, 1776

'...an azure expanse of sea opened to our view,
the domes and towers of Venice rising from its bosom;
innumerable prints and drawings having long since
made their shapes familiar.'

The Travel-Diaries of William Beckford of Fonthill, 1780

Look at this boy.

He is standing next to a blue velvet chaise in the centre of a large room. Apart from a pair of wooden chairs, many footsteps away, there is no other furniture in the space. Instead, the floor stretches out around the boy and he stands alone, like a small pea on an enormous plate.

He considers resting his arm on the chaise but decides not to do so. His chin is hiding in his collar and his hands are behind his back, twisting at his white lace cuffs. He plants his shoes firmly into the floor, locks his knees and looks straight ahead.

A woman is in front of him, next to the window.

'Well, sir, are you feeling worldly yet?' she asks.

The boy glances towards his companion, who is leaning against a wall, far away on the other side of the room. The man's face is scrunched together, forehead and chin almost meeting in pleats near a large red-round nose. The boy cannot tell whether the man's eyes are open or closed.

The boy looks back at the woman. 'No, Signora, I am not yet feeling worldly,' he replies.

The woman smiles and walks towards him. He watches as she approaches with large, loud strides. She holds out her hand. He takes it, just reaching her fingertips.

'It is a pleasure to meet you, Signora Lorenzo.'

'As it is to meet you, Lord Ashcroft,' she says, reclaiming her fingers.

Her hands are rough and dirty and not at all the bejewelled, slender things a lady's hands should be. She has dark smudges on her palms like a chimney sweep and small peeling cracks around her nails.

I am in Venice, the boy thinks, and Reverend Pettigrove told me it is filthy.

The woman has stepped back and is once again assessing the young lord standing in her studio.

'How old are you, sir?' she asks.

'Seventeen in June, Signora.'

'You have beautiful hair,' she says, 'and a neck that is quite, quite elegant.'

Lord Horace Ashcroft stares at the woman for a moment until he realises that he has stopped blinking and an irritating warmth has begun creeping up his face. He drops his chin back into his collar and the quite, quite elegant neck is concealed.

'And such loveleee roseeee cheeks,' Signora Lorenzo adds. 'You are an angel!'

'Oh,' he whispers, his lips barely open. 'Oh.'

She smiles. He swallows.

'And you have very beautiful eyes, Signora,' he manages.

From over near the wall, Reverend Pettigrove loudly coughs.

❧

Lord Horace Ashcroft had decided before he arrived in Venice that this would be the city where he would sit for his portrait. He'd seen many Grand Tour paintings of his acquaintances at home: huge oils that hung like hunting trophies in rooms and hallways across the better parts of Britain. Before he'd left for his own Tour, he often looked at the portraits and felt inspired by the postures of the young men: there they were, in Italy, with all that cultural experience painted confidently across their brows.

Horace particularly admired one portrait of James Fitzwilliam Walter. He was pictured standing, his gaze strong and straight, in front of a window inside a Roman villa. A small grey dog was at his feet, panting up at him with wide perky eyes. Behind the young man, a floating fragment of the Colosseum was visible through the window. Horace appreciated the manner in which Walter stared ahead, disregarding the Roman ruin nearby as though it were as familiar to him as the doting dog. When Horace thinks of that portrait, he cannot imagine himself ignoring the Colosseum in the same way. He doubts whether he could even pretend to do such a thing.

Accordingly, Horace wishes for his portrait to be painted in Venice. The pictures he has seen from this city do not include glorious background antiquities that one is required to disregard. Instead, they feature only the young man himself, and that is how Horace prefers it. He wants his face, his new, open, experienced face, to tell the story.

Oh, to be a man. A real man who has travelled and seen and seized. The craving fills him entirely.

❧

Letter to Samuel Thomas-Sturt, Esq. (aka STS), from Lord Horace Ashcroft, Venice, 1776.

Dear STS,

Upon arrival at the Port of Venice, I was reminded of Canaletto and his canvases of fading light. Those paintings, so revered in Britain, do reflect favourably on the city. They portray a neat Venezia, however, that is entirely inaccurate. The place is a shambles of people and structures and I have already found its vibrancy utterly compelling. The senses are constantly stimulated, my dear friend, and I am oft found gazing like an imbecile at an everyday street scene.

Water laps continually against the buildings and it is difficult to understand how the city remains dry at all. Of course, there are regular floods here, but I understand that the Venetians are expert at managing them.

Upon arrival, we caught a gondola to our lodgings—the Villa di Christo (the home of the most affable Signor Paolo Christo). As we travelled along the immensely busy Grand Canal (akin to Regent Street with water, STS!), I pondered what might be lurking in the depths of the lagoons. Indeed, I was almost expecting a corpse to float by our vessel! Such horror is something I have not chosen to dwell upon.

I have already met with the renowned portraitist, Signora Concetta Lorenzo. She was an excellent lady, quite adept at embarrassing me, and I look forward to further sittings.

I am awaiting the festivities of the Carnival season, due to commence in a week. I have been told that the city becomes utterly dazzling during this period. I imagine, too, that the lewdness you predicted I might witness in Venice will be more fully revealed. Tales of quacks, Orientals and courtesans abound and there are many people already traipsing through the streets in masks. These masks have a profound effect—one has no idea who is behind them, of *course, so a strange anonymity prevails. Rev. Pettigrove has expressed his concern about this. He is convinced that the masks are wholly suspect, providing individuals of dubious character with the opportunity to behave in an appalling manner.*

Rev. Pettigrove is proving to be a somewhat disagreeable companion. He is in a constant state of ill humour and finds an inexhaustible variety of affairs about which to complain. I will not protest any further, however, for fear of being labelled a hypocrite! I wish only to express my ongoing remorse that my preferred companion was forbidden from accompanying me. Your presence on this Tour would have afforded much joy.

I trust that all is favourable in London and your life is not completely desolated by my absence.

I ever am, with regard,
Your most affectionate friend,
Horace

P.S. I saw a marionette in the street today which reminded me of you. It was wearing round spectacles and an immaculate silk coat and had the most glorious waves of dark cotton hair. Very distinguished for a wooden puppet, STS, I assure you!

❧

Horace wakes up with a strange feeling already rushing through him. The sounds of the splashing street echo up into his lodgings and he wonders if perhaps he has heard something dreadful in his sleep: a fight in foreign voices beneath his window, a screaming fall.

Maybe it is simply the water. He cannot understand how such an old, illustrious city can be so alarmingly wet. The very notion of it, lapping away at everything, perplexes him.

Travellers have said that Venice appears to float on the Adriatic, a shimmering fairytale city rising through the clouds. But Horace believes that idea is nonsense: the buildings do just the opposite; they cling to the small section of terrain at their foundations with a crumbling, desperate defiance. They are not floating at all but rather embedded into the earth in a way he has never seen in any other city.

It feels like a constant threat, this teasing water. If a man cannot rely on the very streets in which he walks, what is left for us? Oh, but I am being foolish, he tells himself, dwelling on such things. People have lived in this liquid land for hundreds and hundreds of years.

Today, Horace is going to see some fine examples of the Venetian school of art. Reverend Pettigrove is unenthused about the excursion, believing that there are few commendable artworks in this region of Italy. Horace holds a contrary view. Before leaving England, he was presented with many books on the subject—commentaries written by learned, well-travelled gentlemen that espoused the depth of colour, the vibrancy of the composition, and the often irreverent take on serious subjects that prevailed in Venetian painting. It is the last feature that particularly appeals. Irreverence is a gift, he believes: an important, humanising quality. Horace finds earnest individuals, without the capacity for humour, to be quite abhorrent.

∽

Horace and Reverend Pettigrove step into the gondola that seems always to be waiting at the doorway of their villa. It glides quickly into the centre of the canal as their gondolier, a handsome man with unusually long eyelashes, begins to sing.

His voice is deeply resonant, and he sings without any inhibition, delivering his beautiful tune with the ease of a well-bred lady conversing over tea. Horace wonders if this behaviour is common to all gondoliers: a talent that is synonymous with balancing on a long boat and avoiding the water's traffic. He resolves to use a variety of gondolas throughout the day as a kind of research project into this aspect of local ways.

'It is the most indolent form of transportation,' announces Reverend Pettigrove. 'Look at the people on these boats, reclining as though they were on a lounge in their private rooms.'

'I grant you, Reverend, we could be rowing *ourselves* along the canals, but I prefer the comfort afforded by indolence.'

The boat glides on.

'Do all the gondoliers sing, sir?' asks Horace.

The question is met with a silent frown from his companion.

'Have you noticed all the gondoliers singing, Reverend Pettigrove, or is it a talent unique to our man here?'

The Reverend shakes his head in derision.

Horace sits, shaded by the boat's red awning, with his question still unanswered. He watches the water rushing against the gondola and the occasional colourful surges of accumulated litter. There are so many boats sharing this canal that he finds it extraordinary that he has not yet observed any collisions. Indeed, the view ahead is so crammed with vessels that not a single wave of water is discernible.

Reverend Pettigrove has fallen into slumber. His cumbersome chin provides an ample pillow for the rest of his downturned face, shut to the sensations of the city. The gondolier's voice continues, mingling with shouts and splashes and the most glorious lilting music coming from a small church at the water's edge.

Their boat pulls in at the island of San Giorgio Maggiore.

Lord Ashcroft gives Reverend Pettigrove a small decisive kick as he steps, wobbly, out of the gondola. The Reverend wakes with a grunt before heaving his body onto the solid ground of the bank.

❧

The men admire the façade of the church for several moments: the white marble pillars reflected like a row of long spotlights in the surrounding water; the high dome behind, pushing gently into the clouds. Then they enter and cross briefly through the stately nave, before arriving at the main refectory.

The Marriage at Cana, painted by Paolo Veronese. The huge painting hangs in front of the two Englishmen. Lord Horace Ashcroft is awestruck.

The picture teems with people, with fabric, with musical instruments, with distant towers, with a splendid blue sky and a beautiful terrazzo floor. Horace notes the small dogs in the foreground of the composition: one resting its snout on its paws, the other tugging on its lead, distracted. Irreverence, he thinks, smiling.

'How *very* excessive,' Reverend Pettigrove declares through the silence.

Horace admires the yellow stockings worn by the string player at the centre of the scene and the folds of a brocade tablecloth nearby. 'It is one of the masterpieces of the Venetian Renaissance, Reverend, and painted particularly for this church.'

'Thank you, Ashcroft,' he mumbles, turning away from the picture.

❧

The singing gondolier is waiting for them in his boat at the edge of the island. There are few other gondolas in their proximity and Horace's resolution to change vessels throughout the day is clearly unfeasible. Instead, he decides to question this man directly.

'Excuse me, sir, your singing? Do other gondoliers sing as you do?'

'Not like me, no,' the man says, pushing his boat from the shore.

'You are particularly talented then?'

'*Sì*, sir,' the man says. 'Of course.'

Reverend Pettigrove is sitting at the front of the gondola with a hand at his eyebrows, shading his face from the sun. He looks straight ahead towards the horizon, clearly demonstrating his reluctance to engage in the on-board conversation.

'Did you take lessons, sir?' asks Horace.

'Lessons? No. My mother was a lovely singer and I grew up listening to her voice more in song than in talking, if you understand. She could not talk to people so well, but she could sing like a tiny bird. A tiny bird voice in a big bird woman. But a good tiny bird, you understand—a sweet, clear sound. When I was a little boy, she sang to me always. To help me to fall asleep, to tell me that dinner was made, even sometimes to scold me.'

'So you sing because it is what you have always known?'

'*Sì*, sir, what I have always known. Happy songs on a happy day. Sad songs on days that are not so good.'

'What kind of day is it today?'

'Ah, sir, today is happy.' And with this, the gondolier begins his song once more. He throws his head back towards the sky and his eyelashes close, resting on his face for a moment. Horace looks towards Reverend Pettigrove, whose upper body appears to be swaying along to the tune. It is only a small movement and it may just be the momentum of the waves gently rocking the vessel.

The gondolier sings for the rest of the journey until the boat manoeuvres through a tight canal and slows down beside a large white building lavishly decorated with coloured stone.

'Gentlemen, the Scuola Grande di San Rocco,' he announces.

Later in the afternoon Lord Horace Ashcroft is making an unusual purchase at a market near St Mark's Square: a cutlery set for his mother. Not so strange in itself but the nature of this particular cutlery set has instigated a small quarrel between Horace and his companion.

'What frightful handles,' Reverend Pettigrove declares.

'Not at all, sir,' says Horace. 'They are precisely what I find most attractive about the cutlery. Their colour, you see, it's just like in the paintings.'

Horace has called Reverend Pettigrove away from a bird fancier stall. The Reverend had been regarding a bevy of elaborate displays: a gilded cage containing a pair of cooing quails, a long hanging platform with a raucous parrot and a very large shiny cage enclosing an owl. Reverend Pettigrove looked quite absurd alongside those animals. His rotund red features seemed so rotund, so red, so wholly doughy.

Now the Reverend is standing beside Horace, sneering. 'That blue does not seem entirely appropriate for tableware,' he says.

'It is lapis lazuli, sir. The lady here was explaining that it's worth more than its weight in gold!'

'Ashcroft, please, the *lady* here is trying to sell the items.'

'Reverend Pettigrove, allow me to introduce you to Sophia. She is working today at her father's stall.'

Reverend Pettigrove grunts, nods his head, blinks. Sophia smiles widely and begins to wrap the cutlery. She ties all the pieces together with a cream ribbon, winding the thin fabric many times around the bunch of cutlery before knotting it tightly with a perfect bow.

'Thank you, Sophia,' says Horace, 'that is delightful. My mother will be very pleased.'

'*Grazie*,' the girl says as she takes Horace's pile of coins. She places the wrapped bundle of cutlery in the young man's open hands.

Sophia watches as the gentlemen leave the market, waving goodbye to the boy with the beautiful golden curls. Horace smiles and returns her farewell.

'Lord Ashcroft, it is improper to converse with that class of locals,' says Reverend Pettigrove. 'Say what needs to be said about whatever it is that you are wishing to purchase, but a more comprehensive interaction is entirely unnecessary. While I encourage your gentle communion with the fairer sex, I hope that the next recipient of your attentions will be more appropriate.'

'I beg your pardon, Reverend Pettigrove.'

'You must know you have been completely swindled with the cutlery, Ashcroft! The handles are merely imitation lapis. Did you really believe those mundane objects would be made from such a valuable stone?'

'It was the brilliant blue that I admired, Reverend. If they are merely fakes, then so be it.'

Horace is preparing for bed, exhausted after his day of Venetian revelations. He and the Reverend have just spent several hours playing billiards at a nearby café where they met countless other English travellers, all eager to boast of their wanderings through the city. Horace found that aspect of his day to be particularly tedious: all the tourists, many of them overcome with *vino*, chattering away to each other and attempting to mention some thing, any little thing, that none of their compatriots had noticed. Why is there the incessant need to come together in foreign locales and compete? Lord Horace Ashcroft often wishes that he were the only English milord to have visited this city. He wants the experience all to himself, without comparison or expectation.

He has just placed his new cutlery into a side compartment of his travelling trunk. He is drawn to the objects but has vowed not to look at the glowing blue handles until he takes them to be wrapped for postage.

He gets into bed, blows out the candle at his side and lies very straight in the darkness. The street bustle can still be heard, even at this late hour, and he thinks he can detect a lone voice singing from a far-off place. Lord Ashcroft shuts his eyes and thinks of blue, of paintings, of rushing gondolas, of a man with a cumbersome chin and another man at home in Britain. With an unseen smile, Horace conjures up an alternative Venetian day where his preferred companion replaces the disagreeable Reverend.

The water laps. Softly, and always, against the base of the Villa di Christo.

∽

A few days later, Lord Horace Ashcroft has returned to the studio of Signora Concetta Lorenzo for another sitting.

'Excuse me, Signora, what is that large book?' he asks.

Concetta Lorenzo notes the wrinkles across her subject's forehead and the movement of his pale blue eyes. She glances at the trestle table set up near her easel, seeing the large book in question.

'That is, perhaps, the most important art treatise ever written.'

'A treatise?'

'*Sì*. It is an instruction book for artists. It's full of Renaissance recipes and methods that might have been lost forever if the author had not recorded them.'

'Was the author an artist?'

'Yes, Niccolò de Marco was once a painter. But there was a scandal and he was banished from the guild and became an apothecary. He explains his situation in the treatise's foreword.'

'Did he know very much about your art, Signora? Pastels?'

'He knew a little,' she smiles.

And with this, the conversation ends for a moment and the quiet of her work continues. Lord Horace Ashcroft finds the situation unsettling. Is it acceptable to have protracted periods of silence? Should he be attempting to engage in further conversation?

'Pastel portraits are still quite unusual at home,' he announces.

'Yes,' says Signora Lorenzo. 'Most tourists want oil paintings.'

'Well I do not, Signora. I think your pictures are perfect,' Horace decrees.

'Thank you, sir.'

'They are soft. Like Venice.'

Her drawing stops. 'Soft Venice, sir?'

'Yes, Signora. Even the buildings here do not seem to have sharp edges.'

Signora Lorenzo puts down her pastel and looks at the boy: his white silk stockings, his jade brocade waistcoat, and the dark ruffles that surround his neck like a frame.

'It is easy to lose one's focus here,' Horace continues. 'People seem to get a little lost, as though under a dizzying spell.'

'*Sì*,' encourages Signora Lorenzo.

'And then everything becomes a little blurred. Even the buildings!' He laughs. 'I have seen many travellers tumbling into the canals and I myself have found walking through this city to be a little hazardous. Only yesterday, I slipped on a bridge that was furry with moss. It was without sharp edges, you see! I could barely discern each wooden plank!'

'*Sì*,' nods Signora Lorenzo.

'It is probably due to the sun,' Horace says. 'The strange way it appears to bounce around the entire city. It is never only in one place. It's on the water, the walls, the windows, all at once! It is so beautiful. But with all the mingling reflections here, I doubt that Narcissus himself could find his image.'

'Not even Narcissus, Lord Ashcroft?'

'Not even him, Signora. And in these conditions, how can someone like me not get a little lost?'

'A lord like you, sir?'

'No, a boy like me,' he corrects. 'A boy who can barely recognise himself in the looking-glass above the mantel in his family's own estate. A boy who has been sent on his Grand Tour to . . .'

'Yes?'

'To clarify his manhood.' Horace's gaze drops to the floor near his shining, fidgeting feet.

Signora Lorenzo feels her heart suddenly grow.

'Head up, sir,' she instructs gently. 'I want to see that elegant neck.'

Lord Horace Ashcroft lifts his chin very slowly, his curls folding back into his ruffled collar. His face is a confusion of shame and determined dignity. He sighs and rearranges his features.

'You will be as luminous as Venice, sir,' says Signora Lorenzo as she sweeps a small white pastel across her page.

∼

Letter to Samuel Thomas-Sturt, Esq., from Lord Horace Ashcroft, Venice, 1776.

My dearest STS,

There are so many abominable Englishmen here that it is proving very difficult to escape them. They talk and talk, projecting all manner of unjustified expertise. One could define it as the arrogance of ignorance, that peculiar tendency for a confident person with a miniscule amount of knowledge to find the audacity to project it far beyond its merits.

It really is an oddity of travel—these worldly gentlemen with no ideas. They regard their petty observations as uniquely insightful and spend a good part of their hours in a condition of drunken insensibility. When these visitors are occasionally sober, they dash off to some church or other, as recommended by one of their acquaintances, look inside as quick as a peep and return to the casino to share their freshly acquired knowledge with a pack of gormless milordi.

There are others who view the city as a repository for fascinating data. They are the ones who clutch at books like they are the coat-tails of a local guide, noting the condition of every architectural feature. By memorising each moment of a church's history or acquiring expertise on a style of archway, they behave as though they have conquered the magnitude of all that Venice contains.

So many of the locals speak English here and, of course, I am also practising my Italian. The situation enables an ease of conversation with people throughout the city. It is astounding how a small conversation with a foreigner can be so reassuring. After all, my dear friend, I did not travel to the Continent to fraternise with gentlemen whom I would avoid in my own country!

Forgive me for my ramblings, STS. Sometimes it is necessary to complain, if only to feel relief for having expressed all that has been struggling within. Of course, my impatience with my travelling compatriots is exacerbated by your friendship. When one is aware of an ideal, yet absent, companion, the character of those present is particularly displeasing. I trust that your situation at home is tolerable

*and any talk of redemptive marriage possibilities has been
effectively stalled.*

*I am due at supper in a matter of minutes, so I must
end this correspondence now. I am awaiting a letter from
you, STS, and trust that it is only the dubious postal service
that has prevented my receipt of your words thus far.*

I remain,
Your most affectionate and devoted friend,
Horace

∿

The Carnival in Venice does not start with a sudden and
massive rush of activity, rather the whole city gradually takes
on the garb of the festivities until the colour and noise has
seeped into every small corner and there is barely a space
left to fill.

As Lord Horace Ashcroft steps out of his villa this morning,
he feels it. He sees the frenzy around him and understands
that it is complete; there will be no more acceleration to
the bustle now; it has indeed built up and arrived. The
canals are even fuller than usual—there are people crowded
into gondolas, in some there are as many as ten, shouting
and singing and dressed in Carnival regalia. Their faces peep
out through it all, smiling and exultant.

Horace stands on the stone staircase outside the Villa di
Christo. If he walks down another step, his boot buckles

will be under water. There are no footpaths along this stretch of Venice, just crooked stairs that lead straight into the flowing brown canal.

The singing gondolier is waiting. He is wearing a black cloak and a white half-mask that covers his face from the nose up. His eyelashes can be seen through two holes in the hard fabric disguise and he winks, cheekily, at the young Englishman balancing on the steps.

'Good morning, sir,' shouts Lord Ashcroft. 'I think I need to go on a journey.'

The gondolier nods his agreement and quickly positions the boat against the bottom of the stairs.

Lord Horace Ashcroft steps into the gondola alone, having left the Reverend Pettigrove inside the villa for the first time since their arrival. As the gondolier pushes his oar against the tide, the boat wobbles away and then eases into its rhythm.

'Where is your friend today?' the gondolier shouts over the din.

'He is asleep.'

'Asleep?' the man says, gesturing rapidly. 'There is so much noise, so much to see.'

'Yes!' agrees Horace. 'But he finds all the festivities somewhat overwhelming. He wishes to spend the remainder of the week visiting more of the smaller churches on the islands, but I doubt he will find them agreeable either! He is not used to so much religious decoration, you see. Our churches at home are not so glorious.'

'Ah, *sì*.'

Horace moves a little closer to the gondolier now. He wants to talk to the man without both of them needing to shout.

Another boat pushes past with a group of jugglers balancing inside it. A jester is throwing coloured balls, yelling with satisfaction as he catches them, one after another, in his hands. There is a man holding up a bunch of flaming chariot torches, resplendent against the morning sky. His costume is covered in feathers with a pair of bright yellow sleeves flapping like parrot wings. A small boy sits on his shoulders, twirling a hoop and singing.

The noisy jugglers move away across the canal as Horace settles into a cushion at the gondolier's end of the boat.

'What is your friend's opinion of San Marco?' asks the gondolier.

Lord Ashcroft shakes his head and smiles. 'I do not wish to insult your magical church.'

'Perhaps he says, oh, that blue and gold—it is so . . . vulgar!'

'Yes, that is the word he used!' says Horace.

'Now, sir, where is your mask?'

Lord Ashcroft drops his chin into his collar and blushes slightly. He looks at the gondolier, standing with one leg on the edge of the boat, his Carnival cloak as full as a sail behind him.

'I have not yet put it on.'

'You must, sir. You will find much amusement in disguise.'

Horace reaches into the pocket of his waistcoat and pulls out the white mask he has been carrying with him for several days. He holds it up to his face for a moment and then drops it back onto his lap.

The gondolier offers further encouragement.

Horace lifts the mask towards his face again and with one hand he holds it in place while the other finds the tie to fasten it to the hood of his cloak. Then, reaching both arms behind his head, he secures the disguise. The mask almost covers his entire face; only his bottom lip and chin remain disclosed. The hood is settled over his hair with his curls hidden beneath the heavy velvet fabric.

'I am ready now,' Horace announces.

Upon arrival at St Mark's Square, Lord Horace Ashcroft leaps from the gondola onto the quay and runs into the crowd with rushing people all around him. He runs towards the Doge's Palace, through the Square, past busy stalls and peculiar beasts and coloured costumes and masks, everywhere masks. He dashes to the right around a boxing ring in which two huge men swing punches at each other and everyone shouts, and Horace ducks through the spectators and back into the heaving crowd. He is lifted up now until his feet are not touching the ground. He is being carried along by the people, moving with the press of bodies around him, and he's down, stumbling to find a place for himself, for his legs, just a space among all the others. He runs across puddles with his arms pushing ahead and even the sky is full of ribbons and kites and banners and sun, and he is almost there at the row of arches at the Palace, where the noise is loudest and the colours brightest. And he stops.

He is standing before a magician with black shiny curls, a long purple cloak and a baby white rabbit twitching in a hat. He almost falls onto the man's stall with the momentum of the people pushing behind him, but he looks ahead at the magician's face, white with thick powder and grinning. Horace laughs—his mouth wide open, his shoes gripping the slippery ground, his disguise wrapped tightly around his head with only his laugh to be seen. He is knocked again and turns towards the bodies; he sees two people squealing and dancing along the edge of the crowd, one dressed as Pantalone, the other a small Harlequin with a black-and-white back, moving away and tugging each other through.

'*Buongiorno*!' says Horace, turning back to the performer.

The magician replies with a deep bow and a flick of a red handkerchief that appears beside his lacy cuff. The crowd around the stall cheers the man, applauds his sudden red flourish. The magician grins and spins around and around, stopping finally in front of them wearing a huge blue hat. The crowd gasps.

Behind the magician, a trapeze artist swings past—a boy in green hanging by his knees from a swing tied up high inside the arches of the Doge's Palace. The crowd gasps again. The green child squeals and waves at the people below him and Horace sees that he only has three fingers. Lord Horace Ashcroft blinks, blinks again, straightens his mask and throws his face towards the sky. He shuts his eyes for a moment and listens to the sounds of the Carnival. There are whistles, voices, squeals and a lute, yes, that's what it is, and the constant soft rustle of bodies rubbing past. He opens his eyes, stares at the blue and is relieved that, for a moment, there is only the sky—wide, glowing and familiar. And now a diamond kite flies through the air over his head, and he watches its fluttering yellow tail soar down towards the crowd, watches the curling golden waves disappear.

Lord Horace Ashcroft walks down a narrow alley with his arms stretched out to either side. His fingertips drag across the buildings, gently bumping over stone, peeling paint and furry moss. He can feel that the walls are damp, even the parts that are lit by the sun as it shines in long stripes through the planks of a bridge. He walks along with an uneven stride, stepping on squares of coloured paper scattered along the ground, staring out from behind his disguise.

He has no idea where he is. The maze of Venice has finally consumed him. Other travellers have spoken to him of this risk—the ease with which one can become disoriented in this city. He has been walking through the muddle of streets for quite some time now, moving along, turning corner after corner across the terrain. Once or twice he encountered a small canal lapping at the bottom of a dead-end alley like a heavy barricade he could not possibly traverse. In those moments, Horace simply turned around and continued in a new direction.

I want to be lost, he thinks. I want to have no idea where I am going or why I am going there. He cares only for the movement of his body and the warmth of the air and the delicate moisture touching his fingers.

After an hour or so of wandering, Horace reaches a familiar part of the city, looks up at the pale building in front of him and realises that it is the home of Signora Concetta Lorenzo. Without a thought for social convention, he pulls at the heavy iron handle and opens the door. He steps inside the cool studio and is struck by the smell of pastels.

It is very still and quiet with only a single lamp burning near the easel. Lord Ashcroft tiptoes into the centre of the studio and considers going over to the door of Signora Lorenzo's private rooms to find her. But she steps out now, moving towards her unexpected visitor.

'Lord Ashcroft.'

'*Buongiorno*, Signora.'

'Your eyes are tired, sir,' she comments. 'Have you been enjoying the Carnival?'

'Yes, I have indeed. I must confess that I have only recently left the casino.'

'Of course.'

'There were so many people there, Signora. The English travellers, of course, cavorting with groups of courtesans—all gambling and giggling from behind their disguises. I found myself sharing drink with a group of six gentlemen all wearing identical masks. When two of the men swapped stools and a new person was sitting beside me, it made no difference at all. For me, they were all friends—all instant and neutral friends! It's odd, isn't it, the conversations that occur between strangers when they are free from their own identities?'

'Oh yes. I have watched the Carnival for many years and you are right, Lord Ashcroft. A beautiful face or a frowning face can halt conversation. But a mask is different; a mask allows anything to take place.'

'But how I missed the faces, Signora. I found myself instead looking at hands. Then, of course, there were so many people wearing gloves that I soon grew tired of that. Then I became intent on voices. And even through the chaos of the casino, I could discern some uniqueness in the voices. That was pleasing, Signora.'

'You are very observant, sir. Very observant indeed.'

'I imagine, Signora, that one's tendency to observe is increased by loneliness. That feeling can be most acute when among a crowd, particularly when one's favoured companion is absent.'

'Certainly, sir,' she nods. 'You left a special gentleman at home?'

'Yes, Signora. A very special gentleman.'

'I understand, Lord Ashcroft,' she says with a tender smile.

Horace pulls his mask off his face and shoves it into the pocket of his cream waistcoat. The familiar blush begins to creep across his features.

'Are you aware of the time, sir?' she asks.

He shakes his head.

'The sun rose an hour ago, Lord Ashcroft, and you are fortunate that I usually rise alongside it.'

'Please forgive me, Signora.'

The woman warmly observes the young Englishman in her studio. She looks at his velvet cloak hanging unevenly across his shoulders, the fallen hood crumpled at his neck, his dirty white shoes that are missing a buckle. Horace follows her gaze towards the floor and notices his broken shoe.

'I must look a frightful mess,' he says, ashamed.

'Not at all, sir. You look like a milord at the Carnival.'

'Well,' Horace mumbles. 'Now that I know my whereabouts, Signora, I must return to the villa. I am terribly sorry for arriving here like this.'

'Please don't apologise,' she says. 'As usual, I have found your company most delightful.'

'*Grazie*,' says Horace quietly.

'You must visit me again,' she says. 'I would like to see you one last time before you leave Venezia.'

'Of course,' says Horace, turning to leave.

The woman watches the interesting young man as he stumbles out of her studio into the soft lemon light of the morning.

❧

A couple of days later, Horace has returned to visit his portraitist for the final time.

'I have a present for you, Lord Ashcroft,' Signora Lorenzo says. 'I hope you might be able to fit it into your travelling chest.'

'But you have already given my portrait to Reverend Pettigrove.'

'Yes, but there is something else. Just for you.' Signora Lorenzo guides Horace towards a chair at the edge of her studio. 'Sit down for a moment, Lord Ashcroft.'

She leaves him alone as she retreats into her private rooms. He waits, feeling more like an excited child than is entirely comfortable. He cannot imagine what Signora Lorenzo would be giving him. Perhaps some Venetian glass for his family at home, or a bolt of silk, or even a letter of commendation for the rest of his travels. He waits for her, looking around the studio so his memory of it will be strong.

He sees the wooden floor with some sections that creak. Over there. And there. And sometimes there. He sees the blue chaise he stood beside on the first day he visited. He thinks now of the fraying edge along the front of the velvet upholstery: the tiny tufted fibres that tickled his fingers. He sees the window and the vista beyond; he saw the view once in the morning and he liked it most that way. The canal water was a shivering pink and the white *palazzo* on the opposite bank shone as though it were made of crystal.

He sees Signora Lorenzo's easel and her ledge of pastels: small powdery crayons of varying lengths, each with a working rubbed-down end and a smooth round end. He sees the stub of pale golden brown, almost too small to grasp after his curls were drawn. And he sees the ceiling beams that stretch long across the studio. He is reminded of the moth he once watched up there, flying from beam to beam, playing its own quiet game.

Horace sits very still. Only his eyes are moving, savouring the room.

Signora Lorenzo steps back into the studio. She walks towards Lord Horace Ashcroft, holding a small piece of wood with both hands. She sits down on the other chair and looks at the boy.

'I want to give you a special thing,' she says to him.

Horace doesn't speak nor does he look at what she is holding.

'I have met so many people, Lord Ashcroft, and rarely have they possessed your qualities. You have come from a life of great privilege, yet your soul is quite, quite beautiful.'

'Oh,' says Horace.

'Please be assured, sir,' she continues, 'I have no wish to embarrass you, merely to explain my gift. I am an old woman with a great many connections in this society. I am used to people fussing around me like well-dressed ferrets, talking to me in a manner of excessive tedium. Yet, I have enjoyed your company, Lord Ashcroft. You are a young nobleman, but I believe that you and I see this world in a similar way.'

'Signora, you are an artist. A great—' But his voice smothers itself with shyness.

'Yes. And it wasn't easy to follow my desire for artistry, Lord Ashcroft. I am resigned to a strange life because of this unconventional choice.'

'I see,' Horace manages.

'One must be true to one's heart, sir,' she says.

Horace nods.

'I want you to have this picture. It is three centuries old.'

And now the panel rests on Horace's lap, still and expectant like a pet. He looks down and sees a painting of two cherubs. Simple. Very blue. Rough edges and warping wood.

'Lapis lazuli,' he says at once.

'Oh, sir, you know,' says Signora Lorenzo, delighted.

'Well, I know that,' he replies.

'I have owned this since I was a young woman,' she explains. 'One of my earliest patrons gave it to me after I'd completed a portrait of his son. It had been in his family for many years. Look at the back, Lord Ashcroft.'

With slow adolescent hands, Horace takes hold of the panel and turns it over.

'Caterina,' he reads.

'Yes. A child.'

'It was painted by a child? A girl?'

'Yes.'

'And she was an artist?'

'Well, for a time, yes, Caterina was an artist. Her father was a painter and his twin sons, Giorgio and Segna, inherited his workshop. The Caretto brothers. They worked here in Venice at the end of the fifteenth century. A descendant of theirs was my first patron.'

'But what happened to Caterina?' Horace asks.

Signora Lorenzo takes a moment to reply. 'She died when she was very young. This panel was found later.'

'Oh,' Horace utters, his fingers moving slowly to touch the edges of the painting.

'So, you see,' Signora Lorenzo is saying now, 'it is a special picture. I have waited to meet the right person to pass it to, someone who would recognise its awkward beauty.'

'Oh yes, Signora. It is very beautiful,' he says. 'Thank you so much.'

'Perhaps, one day, you will give it to someone you love. Or perhaps not,' she smiles.

Samuel Thomas-Sturt, Horace thinks, before he should.

Letter to Samuel Thomas-Sturt, Esq., from Lord Horace Ashcroft, Venice, 1776.

To my dearest STS,

Throughout my travels, I have grown to understand that certain expectations are placed upon the Grand Tourist in each city visited. In Rome, for instance, one must engage wholeheartedly with the antiquities of the region. Indeed, antiquities are such the thing in Rome that it is considered almost suspicious to indulge in the city's contemporary society! It is the expectations of the visitor to Venice relating to the conquest of the courtesans that are of particular concern.

I have seen so many courtesans here, brazenly parading in the streets with painted faces and wild floral garments. I find them fascinating, I must admit, but in the manner I find beautiful birds to be intriguing. I have no desire to engage with these women more completely. There is much talk about attaining one's manhood in Venice, STS. Bawdy conversations among the Englishmen here have made that very clear to me. The gentlemen from home are explicit in their commentary on the Venetian female form, discussing physical details as though they were describing the most succulent desserts. Young men are seduced by the courtesans as they ride in their gondolas, or in lavishly decorated boudoirs in crimson corners of the casinos. Indeed, the seductions are as commonplace as the sight of a young beggar in the street. I was, admittedly, startled by this behaviour when I first arrived. Today, it makes me uncomfortable merely because I seem to be alone in my disinterest. Even during Carnival or late at night or after many glasses of wine, my feelings for the courtesans have not become amorous.

There is also a proud display of effeminate manhood here—a bevy of colourful fellows dismissed by most as foppish macaroni. *I find their pride in their own deviancy to be most distasteful.*

I have been unable to relate comfortably with either group and feel quite disheartened. Indeed, as much as I struggle to acknowledge it, my longings have never been directed towards a lady, and yet I feel greatly constrained in embracing an overtly alternative desire.

I am unsure why I feel brave enough to write these words to you. Perhaps it is the safety of distance that perpetuates my brazenness. Perhaps I anticipate an empathetic response. I long for our reunion more than any Continental adventure, knowing that it is in your presence I most fervently belong.

When one is absent from one's home, my dear STS, certain aspects of life become suddenly clear. To continue to exist as one has previously, discarding those revelations, is an irresponsible and foolish endeavour . . .

∾

Lord Ashcroft and Reverend Pettigrove are leaving Venice. They are packing their belongings in preparation for the trip to Switzerland.

'Listen here, Ashcroft,' says the Reverend. 'Some suggestions for packing. I've just found them in the guidebook.'

'What is the advice, sir?' asks the lord.

Pettigrove stands up very straight near the window, the guidebook opened flat on his upturned palms. He looks down at the pages, clearing his throat.

'Clothes are often spoiled in the jolting of a long journey by improper packing,' Reverend Pettigrove reads. 'The buttons ought to be taken off, or at least in folding one side put beyond the other. Flowered velvets are less liable to be spoiled than plain. Books and other hard matters to be packed at bottom.' He closes the guidebook and nods gravely. 'Splendid.'

'Is that all?' asks Horace.

The Reverend looks at the boy, raising his eyebrows and pressing his chins together. 'It is adherence to this kind of detail that ensures a pleasant journey, Ashcroft.'

'Yes, yes, certainly, sir.'

Horace continues to sort his belongings, distributing them into three different piles: soft, foldable items (clothes, handkerchiefs); hard, rigid items (books, notepaper, a *portefeuille* containing maps); odd-shaped, difficult items (shoes, two souvenir fans with tortoiseshell handles, his Carnival mask).

His toiletries have already been packed along with the medicines and directional tools, and Reverend Pettigrove has taken care of the transportation of the pastel portrait.

The Reverend completes his own packing and leaves the room to settle the debt downstairs with Signor Christo. As soon as he closes the door behind him, Lord Horace Ashcroft dashes to the foot of the bed and opens the lid of his travelling chest.

Several days ago, Horace took the blue-handled cutlery from the side pocket and arranged for its postage to England and then, yesterday, he carefully inserted Signora Lorenzo's angel painting in its place. Today, he must decide the most suitable method of transportation for the gift.

He lifts the panel out of the chest, pressing it carefully away from the hard buckles that connect the interior leather flaps. He decides to wrap the painting and chooses the dark velvet folds of his Carnival cloak as a suitable covering. He opens the garment out across the floor and kneels down beside it, puts the panel in the middle of the large black cloak and folds the velvet until the angels are tightly swaddled.

'What did the Reverend say earlier?' Horace addresses the painting, hidden inside the cloak. 'Hard things should be packed at the bottom. Yes.'

So he places the wrapped panel inside one corner of the empty travelling chest, concealing the remainder of the base with books and writing materials. He then covers this layer of hard things with clothes until a messy pile of fabric almost fills the trunk.

But Horace remembers the water—the ocean and its unpredictable surges, the sneaky nature of a puddle washing across the floor of a boat—and he imagines waves full of salty dirt gushing around his travelling chest and the small poplar panel that would be the first thing to feel them if the water seeped into the luggage. So he pulls out the clothes, drops them onto the carpet at his knees and removes everything until the chest is empty once more. He sighs, looks around at his belongings and begins again. This time, he fills the entire chest, grabbing at all the objects scattered across the floor and finishing with a soft pile of clothing: silk stockings, mainly, and a night smock. He pats the fabric, picks up the cloak-covered panel and places it on top of the clothes. It rests comfortably there like a head on a pillow.

Horace can hear footsteps approaching on the staircase. He crashes down the lid of the chest, turns the lock and shoves the key inside his pocket.

Reverend Pettigrove opens the door. 'Ready to depart then, Ashcroft?' he says.

Horace nods and touches his luggage.

Minutes later, their boat trembles away from the port of Venice. The oar is pushed against the base of the shallow lagoon, once, once again, until it stabilises towards the sea.

Horace's travelling trunk is positioned at his feet with both his hands resting gently on its lid. He twists his body towards the city, his eyes scanning the land as it curls further and further away. The din of Venice gradually softens as the sound of the rushing water begins to prevail. Horace looks at the receding buildings and tries to trace their shapes and shadows into his mind. The rooftops make a crooked line against the sky, rising in a multitude of points and curves across the fading expanse of the city. He can see the tower of San Marco—a triangle of grey against the clouds, the angel at its peak just a small golden spot.

The boat slides through the sea, away from Venice. Lord Horace Ashcroft turns his back on the land at last and gazes down into the water beneath him, catching occasional sight of a silvery school of darting fish.

And in the sea, bobbing with the gondola's movement, a portion of papier mâché gently floats. It is a piece of broken Carnival mask—multicoloured with a smeared eye, a stuck-on feather and soft, crumbling edges.

5

It was the Madonna with the green face and the black robe that had started it all.

She was once a Madonna with a pink face and a blue robe, but time had turned her into an ill, Gothic vision. Well, not time so much as people trying to do something about its passing. Arrest eternity, perhaps. Trying to stop a beautiful woman from succumbing to her flaky, fading old age.

She'd been sitting above an altar for three hundred years when the arresting started. Candles had been blowing into her nose for three whole centuries and her face was filmed with the sticky blackness of a fire-fighter in summer. Her eyes were squinty with the floating smoke, yet she was okay.

But then they arrived: the well-meaning conservators who exfoliated her face with acid-soaked rags until the film was gone—and so was her skin. They cleaned her to death, you could say, until the pale green underpaint was revealed like the fresh flesh of a wound.

And her dress, they tried to fix that too. It had once tumbled in blue fabric folds across her body, leaving only two dainty feet and two chubby hands exposed. It had faded and lost a little of its shine, but a good coat of varnish could fix that. Fifty years later, the varnish had turned most of it black with only a few bruises of blue still visible.

And there she was, Morticia-robed and confused, above the altar of a Sienese church. I saw her at the end of a day. I had just wandered into the church and was struck by her strange appearance. You were back at the hostel, after getting shitty and impatient like a child squashed in the middle seat during a car trip. *Are we there yet? How many more paintings can you look at? Why are these streets so fucking steep?* I'd snapped at you like a just-as-grumpy grown-up and kissed you goodbye. Even then, you were intolerant of anything that interested only me.

So I saw her alone. With my camera hanging heavily around my neck and with sticky, over-walked feet. And it didn't take me long to find out why she looked the way she did. To find out that even works of art aren't allowed to age with dignity. A couple of months later, I began my course in art conservation.

Once we came home from our holiday, I stuck a blurry photograph of that Madonna on the frame of my mirror with a ball of Blu-Tack. Sometimes, when I accidentally smeared some lipstick on my chin, I imagined I could see her smiling at me with the dignity of a saint.

❧

You were furious about the study and the fact that I'd failed to fix it. You scolded me in a strangely paternal manner, labelling me irresponsible and lazy.

'Just throw the stuff away. Just get a plumber to have a look at it,' you said, simply.

'I can't. I'm not sure why. I just can't. Anyway, this is your flat too.'

You didn't accept that angle, not for a moment. 'It's always been your domain, the study. It's your junk. Your space.'

That was true: my *junk* filled our home; your realm was really elsewhere, outside our flat, in rehearsal halls or freshly painted studio theatres. I'd warren around that room like a mad old archivist while you shouted monologues into well-lit air.

In my refusal to engage with our minor domestic flood, I was denying the destruction. It's as simple and as complicated as that. Usually you can tell when something has fallen apart. You can see it deteriorating into awkward little pieces and you know, no matter what, it's a broken thing. But, occasionally, it's not so obvious. Occasionally, you find yourself clinging to a fragment that you've mistaken for a whole.

❧

After the removal of the cradle, the panel seemed even more vulnerable. One side was covered in paint; the other side was left bare apart from the section covered by the thin ink brush of 'Caterina'. The exposed back had gained and lost moisture more readily than the front face sealed with paint— contracting and expanding, shrinking and swelling. All that activity had compressed the wood cells and contributed to the natural curve. In the past, conservators did not understand that, in the same way they didn't understand that pure alcohol was a ruthless solvent or that a slap of resin varnish would rapidly discolour, or even that it might be a bit problematic to cover a figure with a modest robe centuries after the artist had painted it nude.

But the curl was to remain in the panel; I was not going to try to yank it flat. The old attempt to do so, with the attachment of the heavy cradle, had caused the poplar to split along the grain.

So I filled the gaps. With a strong adhesive and a gentle push, the curved piece of wood became whole once more.

Once the painting's support was stabilised as much as possible, the cleaning of the image began. It was a long, often tedious, process. Sometimes, I wished I could just wash the entire painting: grab it like a grimy dinner plate and wipe it with a sponge, detergent foaming across the blue. Instead, I worked with a brush, its bristles so soft I could barely feel them on my fingertips.

I filled a container with de-ionised water and touched the brush against the meniscus. I held my breath as I cleaned the paint layers, placing the brush on the image with a butterfly lightness. On the more stable sections, I used a cotton-covered satay stick, swabbing it across the paint. Sometimes, I used my own spit to dislodge the grime—a common practice that startled non-conservators in the way a diner can be distressed by the sight of a chef mixing food with her hands.

Slowly, the true colour of the painting was revealed. A millimetre at a time.

As I cleaned the cherubs, I talked to them—I muttered quietly about how gently I would treat them, that my intention was only to hold them together, not transform them into a false perfection.

I wish I had explained to you how engrossed I was in those procedures. This is what I might have said. You know what it feels like to get off a plane in a tropical country, Singapore perhaps? How the humidity is so thick that you become aware of your own breath? And so something as mundane as breathing becomes a revelation. The panel affected me in a similar way. *I'm working. I'm working*, I kept thinking after it arrived, as though that was something I had never done before.

I continued, touching its layers, until I bumped a beaker beside me with my elbow. The water inside came perilously close to spilling out. I grabbed the glass, swore loudly and watched the liquid stabilise once more.

I realised then that there wasn't any existing water damage on Caterina's panel. I searched again for bubbled paint layers. I looked for a patina of salty residue on the cherubic curves, like the film that clings to skin after a dip in the ocean. But neither was evident, as I already knew. For five hundred years, the panel had been protected from any menacing liquid. While that wasn't necessarily strange, it struck me and made me paranoid. I glanced up at the fire sprinklers dotted across the ceiling of the lab, glared at their white spiked spirals poised to emit their spray, and willed them never to lurch into action. The weight of history hit like a pendulum, knocking my composure away.

I took off my apron and crossed the lab towards Gillian. She was working on a latex sculpture. It was a young artwork, less than twenty years old, and it appeared to be rotting. The object—a group of seemingly random shapes connected by rope—trailed across the table. When it was made, the latex would have been translucent and flexible and it had since decayed into a state of opaque rigidity. I wondered if the material's evolution was intentional, if the effect of time had been included as a curious component of the object, as intrinsic as the rope or the rubber.

'Is that even meant to last?' I asked her.

'Well, we have to try,' Gillian said. 'The client's paid for it to be restored.'

'And the artist?'

'Dead.'

'Oh.'

'You know what it's like. When artists started working on canvas, people had no idea how to conserve that material. Wood was okay, walls were okay, but fabric, *oh no*.'

'But techniques developed because everyone wants everything to last forever.'

'Yep,' she laughed. 'Even if we just prevent complete disintegration. For the moment.'

That night, you came home with a gift, and I began to hate you a little. I walked into our flat, into our bedroom, and there you were, sitting cross-legged and adorable on our bed.

'What's that?' I asked, leaning over to kiss you. There was a present at your feet, wrapped in generic shop paper—neat and unadorned green.

'It's for you.'

'Who from?'

'From me,' you said. 'Sit down.'

I sat on the edge of the bed and you pushed the small flat parcel towards me. It shunted slowly across the doona like a decrepit train carriage. I reached towards it.

'Wait, wait,' you said.

I untangled the lapis lazuli bracelet on my wrist and folded my hands together.

'Because you must be almost finished with the panel painting by now—' you began.

'Well, no, not really.'

'Anyway, it'll be soon—'

'Mmm.'

'Well, because you'll be finished with it one day,' you continued, 'I thought I'd get you this. So you'd remember it.'

I picked up the gift and peeled off the sticky-tape. It was a book. A small, white, hardcover book. I turned it over.

'*Love Angels*,' I read.

'Open it,' you instructed. 'It's all pictures. Of angels. There was a whole series of books. Some with baby animals, some with famous Hollywood couples. And this angel one. They're very cute. In pairs mostly. Like the painting.'

I flipped through the glossy pages.

'Like the painting?' I said.

'Yeah.'

I tried to think of a way to explain the difference between Caterina's panel and those tacky little images, between something I loved and something cropped and packaged by a gift company. I looked at you, so happy with your offering, and I didn't say a word. Instead, I carefully tore a page from the book—a detail of Raphael cherubs—and lodged it in the edge of my mirror. You were pleased, I remember, although a little concerned about the torn page. I reassured you that my mirror was the perfect place for that picture, and explained that I could hardly wedge the entire book into the frame. The old ravaged face of my Madonna was obscured by the new glossy page from *Love Angels*, both of them adding to the collage that covered the glass and distracted me whenever I tried to inspect my own skin.

We made dinner together then and made conversation too. I went to bed early, feigning exhaustion, and dreamt of the fish family surviving the flood. When I awoke in the middle of the night, I lay there and peered at you for some time.

Eventually, you woke up also, sleepily reaching under my t-shirt. The sex. Well, that hadn't wavered.

Sex with you was different to anything I'd ever known. Or imagined. It certainly wasn't the sort that just started with kisses, and turned into clothes peeling, bit of boob grabbing and whammo, in ya go. It wasn't even close to that kind of target-the-erogenous-zones bonking. It was every part of us, all at once. Nothing was untouchable, un-lickable. Remember, at the beginning, when you tried to kiss the arch of my foot and I kicked you in the mouth? But you insisted and persisted until I let you kiss my feet and soon there wasn't anywhere we didn't go. We'd spend hours kissing each other's legs and armpits and backs and bits, places that I never thought I'd desire on someone else's body, places that I never thought would be desired on my own. You could look at my elbow, my bony, dry-skinned elbow, like it was the sexiest thing you'd ever seen.

I still think of it, occasionally, and wonder if you were with someone else, later on.

But we'd stayed there in sex and shut down in the rest of the relationship and I couldn't handle the difference. I suffered the common misapprehension that one should be a reflection of the other. That night, I stopped and asked you about it—the discrepancy—and you answered with a bloody quote from Tennessee Williams.

'It's like in *Streetcar*. Stella has that awesome line: "There are things that happen between a man and a woman in the dark—that sort of make everything else seem—unimportant."'

I considered those words. 'Isn't that about the crap you accept in daylight because of the lust that exists when you go to bed?'

'Nooo. It's about the bond between lovers because they do things together that they don't do with anyone else,' you said, grabbing my face.

With the distance between us, I think I would've preferred eyes-closed, heartless fucking to the adoring intimacy that had continued. At least that would've made sense to me. At least that would not have seemed so pathetically out of synch. So I rolled away from you. I wasn't interested in the pretence. I didn't believe it meant a thing.

I recognise now that that night you gave me the book was one of our final attempts at being together.

At the start of a relationship, I think a person can recognise the shifting moment when genuine intimacy arrives. And it also happens at the end. In increments. Down, down, down you go until the gears have moved so far that you are safe enough to turn the corner into somewhere new.

That is what I'd thought. That we were safe enough to move.

∽

I returned to the panel and by the end of that week I had finished the cleaning process. I had removed hundreds of years of accumulated dirt. The painting shone—the blue hue and those wings, suspended in its vapour. But like any surface cleaning, the fresh exposure also revealed the painting's more fundamental problems. What remained was a flaking picture: a mottled ultramarine sky and a pair of peeling angels with delicately expansive wings. And there was a mesh of subtle cracks across the entire painting—the craquelure— as though it were being viewed through a piece of shabby flywire.

The craquelure is a sign of the inevitable aging of the image layer. It's like the laughter creases on the old face of a happy person: an acceptable anomaly. A painting is not allowed to flake, it's not allowed to fade, but it is allowed to softly crack. To quietly sign its age in the finest lines like ink.

Those lines on the wings were beautiful. They drew the tiniest feathers across the span as though age had revealed more detail. There was a soft web of craquelure across their bodies too. Wispy wrinkles like the loose tissue-paper skin of the aged.

After cleaning, before retouching, the craquelure on the panel was wholly visible. And unlike the flaking layers and the faded pigment spots, those cracks would remain on the painting.

6

~

PARIS, 1877

'What was Art, after all, if not simply giving out what you have inside you? Didn't it all boil down to sticking a female in front of you and painting her as you *feel* she is?'

EMILE ZOLA, *The Masterpiece*, 1886

Look at her back in the mirror.

Her small torso is heaving with exertion and a trickle of perspiration follows her spine into her corset. The layers of creamy tulle in her skirt puff out from the waist, falling to the top of her calves. The material is heavy around her legs and she holds it up and away from her body for a moment. Her head is bent forward, looking at the wooden floor, as she stands silent at the edge of the studio, breathing in and out in time to the music.

'Elise Halévy!' shouts Madame Zappelli.

'*Oui*,' the dancer replies. '*Pardon*.'

And she moves away from the mirror, running forward with her feet sticking out to the sides. She steps into a soft *arabesque*—the perfect position appearing from her body in an instant.

'*Un. Deux. Trois*,' says Madame Zappelli, and the old man on the chair in the corner begins to play his golden violin once more.

Elise dances alone at the front of the room. There are eight other girls far behind her who move to complement the *étoile* as she glides through the *adage* created for her by the old ballerina watching with her gaunt, pinched face quivering in suspense. Elise glances at Madame Zappelli as she extends into a *développé devant*. The old woman stares at Elise's legs and the young dancer sees that her face is hard. As usual, Elise knows that Madame Zappelli is expecting her to wobble or falter in some way until she is left crumpled over like a puppet whose strings are suddenly released. But Elise does not wobble; only an ant running across the boards would be able to see her left foot gently shaking as it grips the floor. Her other leg is suspended in the air for a single note and is now gently lowered into a *retiré* at her knee. Elise thinks of her foot and pushes the heel forward a little as she points it.

She has perfect feet. That's what the other girls say, and Madame Zappelli and many of the subscribers to the Opéra, in their attempt to understand what is important to the dancers. You have such perfect feet, an aristocrat will say to

Elise after overhearing the girls ooohing at her arches. And then, later, he might see Elise's blistered toes released from their *pointe* shoes and wonder why he has complimented her.

Elise is coming up from her final *arabesque penchée*, rising a little quicker than she would like just to keep up with the music. But the violin slows and she smiles gently as she finishes dancing. She raises her arms into the closing position, lifting her fingers gradually for the whole length of the violin's bow.

'*Bon*,' says Madame Zappelli.

Elise relaxes and looks gratefully at the old man in the corner with his violin on his lap. He nods at her with a grin.

'Not bad, Elise,' says Madame Zappelli.

She stands up to discuss one section of the *adage* after dismissing the other dancers from the studio. Elise watches Madame Zappelli demonstrating the steps. While she admires the strength left in her legs and her undeniable aplomb, the younger dancer can see no beauty in the retired ballerina. It is not because she is old; it's the lines on her face that her life has given her. So many frowns, deeply embedded like cuttings in clay—frown under frown—all pointing in sharp arrows towards her mouth. Just smile, thinks Elise, just smile and your face won't become so mean.

'What are you grinning about, Elise?' snaps Madame Zappelli.

'Nothing, Madame.'

And with this, Elise begins to dance again, concentrating on maintaining her flawless line and remembering not to smile.

&

An hour later, Elise is sitting on an omnibus heading home to her parents' shop on Rue Clauzel. She is leaning slightly out of the window, enjoying the breeze on her face and the sound of the plane tree leaves occasionally brushing against the side of the vehicle. She lurches to the left as the big yellow bus turns a corner and a splash of gutter water momentarily covers the wheels.

Elise's journey home is only a brief one yet it gives her time to simply sit and think, usually about the work day she just manages to leave behind in time for the start of the work night and her performance: the tensions she experienced with whispering dancers or batty teachers, or the strategic seductions of the Opéra subscribers. Those straight-backed men, experts on money in one way or another—stockbrokers, investors, aristocrats—who watch performances from the best boxes in the theatre and fraternise with each other at the top of every staircase in the building. Over the years, Elise has tolerated her personal group of aficionados, usually comprised of men who think that detailed accounts of their own business dealings make for alluring flirtation.

Currently, Monsieur Theodoras Malikas is the most eager candidate. An enormous Greek diplomat who has only been a Parisian resident for the last few months, he is known amongst the dancers as the 'big man with the big hat', or 'Elise's Theo' because of his appearance at the door of her dressing room after every performance. He has a cheery knock-knockety-knock that is immediately recognised by Elise and her dresser. And after the knock, M Malikas waits. He likes to stand there, all six foot four of him, leaning casually on the doorframe with one leg kicked out in front. When the door to the dressing room is opened, he straightens himself up and steps inside with his hand on the brim of his black top hat, smiling his greeting.

Elise likes him well enough. He is far nicer than some of the other gentlemen who traipse through the theatre's corridors and rooms as though it were their own dancer-filled *château*. Most of all, she cannot tolerate the ones who wink from beneath their hats. Winking, she thinks, is appropriate only with children. As a means of seduction, it is absurd. M Malikas also seems to be genuinely enamoured of the dancing itself, not merely of the social opportunities to be found at the Opéra. He is one of a few regulars at their rehearsals and sometimes he arrives, watches and leaves the studio without speaking to anyone at all. Yes, she likes him well enough.

The omnibus turns into Elise's street, passes the barber and the herbalist and pulls to a stop in front of the fruit shop. She gets up and stands at the door of the vehicle for a moment, perched on the step with one foot pointing straight to the gutter. She jumps onto the ground outside, her legs bending with considerable soft grace as she lands. She waves quickly at the fruiterer in front of her, a young man who almost drops a sack of small red apples at the sight of the ballerina. Elise laughs quietly to herself, throws her tapestry bag over her shoulder and begins the brief walk down Rue Clauzel.

Elise soon arrives beneath the familiar sign on her home: '*Halévy—Marchand de Couleurs*'. She goes inside, taking care not to bump any of the shelves near the doorway and lowering her head slightly to avoid the bunches of brooms hanging from the roof above her. The shop bulges with stock, crowded so snugly that a single careless swing of a coat would send things toppling.

Elise's parents are standing with a group of customers around the central shop counter. Her father is flipping through a paint manufacturer's catalogue while the customers make judgmental noises at the sight of each new page. Elise's mother watches the proceedings, piping in regularly with smooth words of persuasion.

'Now that—that is an unusually clear yellow. We're very excited to be stocking it, aren't we, Claude?'

'Oh yes,' her husband replies.

Elise moves towards the rear of the building. She smiles at her parents as she slides quietly into the darkness of their private rooms. A golden Japanese screen shields the doorway, its strong diagonals almost directing her away from the shop.

'That's our daughter,' Elise can hear Claude saying to the customers. 'She's a ballerina at the Opéra.'

Elise cannot discern their reply.

She will spend the next couple of hours preparing eight pairs of *pointe* shoes for the evening's performance. It's a tedious task that involves sewing on sixteen slippery lengths of pink satin ribbon with the tiniest, tightest stitches, banging the toe of each shoe on the ground for several minutes to blunt the edge and diminish its noise and, finally, inserting an extra strip of wood into each sole to support her bulging arches.

Blanche has just completed a new display in the front window of the colour shop: a large promotion for synthetic ultramarine. She is concerned about the drop in the pigment's sales after its initial popularity several years ago and has decided to encourage a revival in its usage.

She has covered a small artist's palette with synthetic ultramarine and placed it next to an old panel painting she recently acquired from an artist as part-payment for supplies. She accepted the panel from him precisely with this purpose in mind. The small painting, although amateurish, provides an ideal example of the old pigment that contemporary chemists have worked so hard to emulate.

She has made two small signs—one reading: *Genuine Ultramarine (Renaissance pigment made from lapis lazuli)*, and the other: *Synthetic Ultramarine (modern pigment available here*)—and placed them beneath the panel painting and the palette. A third sign hangs above the two blue objects: *Can you tell the difference?*

Blanche has a knack for this type of thing. She was the first colour merchant in Paris to stock boxes for outdoor painting. Small cases, she'd thought a few years earlier, that's what the artists need for their excursions to the Forest of Fontainebleau. Blanche soon found a supplier of wicker baskets, like picnic hampers with soft fabric lining, which the painters purchased in droves. Nowadays, there are specially manufactured outdoor painting kits, complete with collapsible canvas stools and thin leather straps for easy carrying, available at every colour merchant in the city.

When a new type of charcoal became available last year, Blanche found an artist to demonstrate it inside the shop's front window. She paid the man five francs for the week and provided him with enough charcoal (and reams of low-grade paper) to draw continually for as long as the store was open. The idea was very successful and they sold more boxes of charcoal than any other shop in Paris.

This ultramarine display is particularly notable and Blanche is standing on the footpath admiring it, just as Etienne Robert turns the corner from Rue des Martyrs and arrives at the shop door.

'Good afternoon, Madame.'

'Ah, Etienne. Still in Paris, I see.'

'*Evidemment*,' he replies with a patient smile. 'I still long to leave for the country, but there's much to organise.'

'Of course, of course.'

Etienne glances at the window where two cherubim fly at the centre of the old blue panel. Their wings have caught his eye.

'Now, what have you run out of today?' Blanche asks her customer.

Together, they walk inside the colour shop to arrange his purchase of a tube of chrome yellow, another of rose-pink lake, and three standard lengths of pre-stretched, woven linen.

The young artist leans on the shop's counter, leafing through a nearby pile of thick watercolour papers, while Blanche collects his supplies.

As he receives his order, he compliments the shopkeeper on her latest impressive window promotion. 'I like the panel painting in the window, Madame,' he says. 'It really is the most magnificent blue.'

'Yes,' she concedes. 'But the synthetic is just as pleasing. That's what I'm trying to display.'

'I understand, Madame, but that genuine ultramarine is so rare and those wings are simply—'

'It's an average little panel. Don't you think, Claude?'

Blanche's husband is fussing around the shop, moving full pots of bristle brushes from one shelf to another. He turns towards his wife and their customer.

'I haven't given it much thought. But I'm sure you're right, my dear.'

The young artist and Claude exchange smiles as Blanche scrutinises her new display again. From inside the store, only the blank backs of the three small signs are visible. That looks a bit drab, she thinks. I may have to work on it a little more.

'I think the panel painting is rather beautiful,' announces Elise Halévy, emerging from behind the Japanese screen. 'Those angels don't have a care in the world.'

And with this, Elise walks across the store, effortlessly avoiding its countless products, through the front door and into the street.

'Who is she?' Etienne asks. What an incredible face, he thinks. He wants to chase after her, run like a madman from this cluttered little shop and seize her.

'That is our daughter, Elise,' smiles Claude. 'She's a ballerina at the Opéra.'

'Oh.'

Blanche looks at the young artist, shakes her head at his tatty shirt and his glowing eyes. 'She has many suitors, Monsieur, many suitors indeed.'

Several hours later, Etienne is standing beneath one of the archways at the façade of the spectacular Opéra house. He is leaning against the cool stone column at the top of the steps, a safe distance away from the afternoon traffic shifting across the Boulevard des Capucines and the Place de l'Opéra intersection. His eyes are closed to the sight of the bustle as he enjoys the sounds around him and the coldness of a shadow on his body. This is one of his regular activities: deliberately shutting down one sense and focusing instead on the satisfactions of the others. If the people sauntering past the Opéra were to glance in his direction, they might scoff at the scruffy young man under the arch: his casual dress and stance, his serene face—still and smiling—in the middle of a city where so many people are harried.

Earlier, Etienne accosted a young dancer, one of the junior 'rats' in the company, regarding the whereabouts of Mademoiselle Halévy.

'She is still in rehearsal, Monsieur,' came the timid reply.

'For how much longer?' he shouted to her bobbing, departing head.

'I cannot say, Monsieur. Elise is the *étoile*, you know.'

Of course she is, Etienne thought. Of course, the girl with the unforgettable face is the star of the Opéra; her presence in the *corps de ballet* would be far too distracting. Etienne has only seen two Opéra performances but he can understand that much about its dancers.

The small conversation with the 'rat' took place almost an hour ago and Etienne is still waiting for Elise to emerge. Fortunately, there is no other part of Paris where he would rather spend his idle time. Etienne leans into the stone façade of the Opéra as though it were a familiar and much-loved person. He has adored this building for as long as he can remember; he even defended the design when so many other people found the project to be most disagreeable.

'It's gaudy. It's cumbersome,' his artist friends declared, only days after the first columns were lowered into place.

'It's courageous,' Etienne insisted. 'Just wait until it is finished. Imagine if the people of Paris stood beside you, critiquing every brushstroke as you painted. That's what you're all doing here. Every brick is being assessed and the building is still being built, my friends! It's unfair to judge a work of art when it's in the midst of creation.'

When it finally opened, the public was very proud of the Opéra's wedding-cake confidence and naturally Etienne's friends wanted to dislike it even more once it became so popular. After all, they were bohemians; it wouldn't do for their tastes to correspond with those of the masses. Etienne laughs at this memory now, just as Elise dashes down the steps in front of the archway where he is waiting.

'Mademoiselle,' he shouts as soon as he sees her.

Elise stops on the bottom step and turns towards the voice.

'*Oui*?' she says, her face frowning against the glare of the lowering sun.

'I saw you today,' he says, venturing slowly down towards her. 'At your parents' shop. My name is Etienne Robert. And I am a painter.'

'Hello, Monsieur,' she says. 'My name is Elise Halévy. And I am a ballerina.'

They are standing side by side on the same stone step. Elise tilts her head slightly and admires the young artist. What beautiful eyes, she thinks. Dark and clear and unafraid to dwell.

'Do you have time to stop at a café with me, Mademoiselle?' Etienne asks.

Elise shrugs her shoulders. 'Well, yes, I do.'

And together they walk off down the street with their arms occasionally brushing as they swing and their matching long strides slicing through the dawdling crowds.

The following week, Elise has an afternoon free of rehearsal. She is standing in Etienne Robert's freezing studio, intently watching the painter as he steps out from behind the easel between them.

Initially, Elise was rather coy. She stood on the step outside the building for a moment, teetering at the entrance like a child approaching a suspension bridge. She wanted to stride into this strange adventure but she wasn't entirely sure if she could trust it. The painter seemed nervous too. He told her that he'd never before used a dancer as a model, and when she was changing her clothes behind his dusty old curtain, she could hear him pacing, back and forth, on the other side of the studio. But now she is standing where she was told, against the far wall of the room. She is in her rehearsal clothes, as Etienne requested, and he is drawing her—just charcoal sketches at this stage, quickly executed on hastily discarded sheets of paper.

'Do you want me to do a *tendu*?' Elise asks.

'Pardon?'

'Do you want me to point my foot in front, like this?' she asks, demonstrating the movement.

He looks at the sudden arch of her foot and her calf muscle, so strong and rounded, inside the palest pink stocking.

'No. I would like you just to stand there.'

There is a moment's silence as the artist and his subject recognise the advantages of this situation, allowing them to stare at one another with an intensity that would be unacceptable in normal circumstances. The portrait sitting elicits a strange acceleration of intimacy; they have been together in this studio for only minutes and already she has noticed the contours of his hands and he has observed the shape of her ears: small lobes atop a long, proud neck.

'It's so unnatural, isn't it?' Etienne says.

'What's unnatural, Monsieur?'

'Ballet.'

Elise thinks for a moment and shakes her head. 'Well, no,' she says, adjusting a sleeve. 'To me, it doesn't seem that way.'

She has never considered the 'naturalness' of ballet. For her, it is the only thing she has ever known; she doesn't remember making a deliberate choice to dance. She was sent to her first class when she was eight years old and, from that day on, was told that she was perfect for ballet. It has been ten years of compliments now, affirmations of her talent by every teacher and choreographer that she has encountered. Not once has she thought to question it. Even when she is exhausted or bored or nervous, she does not question it. The realisation makes her feel rather foolish.

She looks at Etienne—this handsome young man so enthralled by his own ideas—and wonders if he realises the impact of his comment.

She turns her head towards the row of grimy little windows running down one side of the room and sees the clouds of the afternoon being pushed along by the wind. I must remember to notice those things more often, she thinks; I'd forgotten that the clouds even move at all.

Etienne glances up from Elise's waist and focuses on her face. Her animated black eyes, her wide red lips, and her nose, a touch aquiline and sometimes slightly twitching in a way she probably doesn't realise. Her cheeks remind him of a cherub's. They are the roundest part of her body. Well, almost, he thinks, with a sudden look at the soft cleavage pushing from her bodice. He is smiling at her, smiling at her with his eyebrows up and his chin down and his gaze, warm and lusty, directly on her face. But now he sees her expression. Her eyes are especially large and round, and her mouth is tensely closed.

'Are you alright, Elise?' he asks.

'Of course.'

'No, you're not. You're sad.'

'Why do you say that?'

'Because your face hides nothing. It's utterly transparent.'

Elise looks at Etienne and smiles pleasantly. It's okay, it's okay, she tells herself. Just smile. 'I have been told that I am a fine actress, Monsieur. Many times.'

'Oh, I have no doubt that, on stage, you are a wonderful actress. It's just that, in life, you can forget to use those skills.'

Elise laughs at the man standing in front of her. At his audacity, his baggy threadbare trousers, and his bristly olive skin that she suddenly yearns to touch.

They start in frozen doll-like positions for this section of the ballet. Elise is standing downstage, centre. In front of her is the darkness of the auditorium and the sudden hush of the crowd as the heavy velvet curtains sweep open. Below her, she sees the conductor's baton rise in the air as it flicks neatly to the opening bars of music. She begins to dance. Spot, spot, she says to herself as she pirouettes, finishing in a neat lunge with her arms forward as if to embrace the air, reach to the audience, draw the darkness into her world. Her dress swings around her legs after she has stopped spinning, the momentum of the fabric almost pulling her over. But she is strong; her feet stick to the ground when required and push off into the air when they need to. And she can appear as light and lilting as a flower petal being blown across a lawn while her stomach muscles are clenching to hold her upright. The roar of applause from the audience vies with the music and she smiles; with every tendon in her body, she smiles.

After a ten-minute sequence with a prince and a parade of peasant girls, Elise's section is finished. She dashes backstage, brushes against the edge of a scenery canvas and stops next to the heavy stone wall in the front corner of the wings. A small familiar sign, stuck to the stones with an old dollop of eyelash glue, is right in front of her: *Do not adjust your minds*, she reads. *There is a fault in reality.* Stay in that world, she thinks. Dwell in it.

So, obediently, Elise follows the sign's suggestion. She turns towards the stage again and watches the dancers jumping softly through a lush forest of cardboard foliage. They are lit by rows of humming gas lamps that make their skin glow like glass.

Later, Elise is asleep in her old single bed at the rear of the colour shop. If she hadn't been living here all her life, she might have noticed the paint and turpentine odours in the air. She's wearing a white cotton nightgown that hangs all the way to her ankles when she stands up in her bare feet at the foot of the bed. But now she's cocooned in two woollen blankets and a sheet, with her head on a pillow that's always belonged to her. It's lumpy and squashed around her face, just the way she likes it. Placed, as always, with an old stain from a nosebleed on the bottom left corner. This way, the shape is the same for her each night as she snuggles into sleep. Lying flat on her front, her head to the right, her plait of hair resting behind her like a long silky animal across the pillow, she's sleeping.

Etienne, streets away in his poorly lit studio, is not asleep. Instead, he is ravaging a canvas with rapidly twisting brush-strokes. After more than a month of modelling sessions with Elise, he has begun work on a series of oils: ephemeral, soft paintings of weightless ballerinas shrouded in mist and wan, weary light. He is excited, inspired, eager to show a finished work to the beautiful dancer who has begun to preoccupy him completely. His usual concerns—submitting an acceptable work to the Salon, arranging a move to the country—have become overshadowed by his desire to impress his friend.

She will love this, Etienne thinks. My paintings will delight her.

❧

'Guess what my mother said before I came here today?' Elise asks Etienne.

'I don't know. Tell me.'

'She said—I hope that artist is decent, Elise. Those types are not always decent.'

'Decent?'

'Yes,' she laughs. 'And what's so amusing is that every time I set foot inside the Opéra house, there is a swarm of "gentlemen" around me and I have to concentrate, literally concentrate, on managing their attentions. But, of course, she doesn't understand that!'

'Did you defend my decency, Mademoiselle?'

'Oh no. I gave no reply.'

The painter takes Elise's hand and leads her to the easel in the centre of his studio.

'Shut your eyes,' he says. He looks at his painting, quickly grabs his palette, adds a dab of white near a foot. 'You may look now.'

Elise opens her eyes, takes one step back from the easel and glances across the canvas, down the canvas, as though reading a giant page of words.

'Well?' he says, his patience gone.

'It's pretty, Etienne.'

'Pretty,' he repeats.

'Why is it that portraits of men are made to honour them and portraits of women are made only to admire?'

'I don't understand.'

'This picture. That is not me. That's how you might like to think of me, but I don't look like that when I'm in rehearsal. My hair isn't neat, I have never worn a pair of earrings that large and I do not smile.'

'Oh?'

'I don't smile like that. If you want to paint something interesting, perhaps you could paint the ballerina in the studio who does not smile.'

'Why don't you smile?'

'Etienne, if you want to paint angels, you should paint them. But if you want to paint me, please don't diminish me or make me prettier and easier to admire. If you painted a man, would you go to so much trouble to lighten his character?'

'No,' admits Etienne.

Elise storms over to one of the small windows and glares outside.

'The very last thing I intended was to diminish you,' Etienne says. He puts down his palette and walks to her.

He takes both her hands and holds them to his chest, pressing them against his paint-covered shirt. He is relieved that she doesn't resist the gesture.

'I am so sorry,' he begins. 'You have so much character and I didn't know how to paint it. How can I? How can I paint your strength and your grace, all your beauty, all at once?'

She shrugs slightly, wanting more.

'So I just ignored it all and made you an angel. Because they're simpler. And I'm a fool.'

Elise looks up at the face of the man clutching her hands, squeezing them tightly. So it's happening, she thinks. The moment when everything shifts. And she is surprised at the problem in it—the confusion that is pushing them together. She breathes, focusing on him and his worried lips.

'Etienne?' she says slowly.

'Yes?'

'I think I love you. And I thought you may have loved me too—'

'I do—'

'—but when I looked at that painting, I thought, no, he just thinks I am pretty, like all those men at the Opéra. He isn't different. He doesn't see as much as I thought.'

'No, Elise,' he says. 'That's not true. I do love you for your beauty, yes, but for so much more. I adore you and I know you. I promise.'

'It's alright,' she smiles. 'I believe you.'

She pulls him close, their tangled-together hands released and reaching. And they kiss—their mouths open to each other with a desperation that is far from decent.

&

They are lovers immediately. Their lives become things to lead when they aren't able to be together. That's how it feels for them both. Her dancing, his painting—the passion has moved a little away from those things and found a different place to land.

Sometimes, when she is on stage, Elise makes a decision to think only of Etienne, to imagine that the auditorium only contains him and that the prince of the ballet whose arms will catch her over and over is Etienne, and the rest of the dancers and the scenery and the costumes are all Etienne, until she is completely enveloped by him and she jumps higher and spins faster and balances longer with the strength of his presence. When she leaves the stage she carries that feeling with her, down the dank twisting corridors of the theatre, into the cushioned chair of her dressing room where she meets M Malikas with an effortless floating courtesy. With the same serenity she removes her make-up, smells bouquets of flowers, peels off her costume and covers herself in street clothes. It even seems as though her body aches less after a performance now, as though this big encompassing love has made everything easier.

She leaves the Opéra quickly after each performance, reunites with Etienne at a café far enough away from the swarming audience members—the flirtatious subscribers and the ladies in tight bright coats—and embraces him until they are both gasping for breath. Each night they sit together in the café, leaning over the small round table towards each other—covering the whole surface with their arms—talking and laughing and kissing until something like tiredness makes them retreat.

That is how it has been for months now. Until tonight.

Elise arrives at the café at the usual time and Etienne is not there. Instead of grabbing her lover, she orders a glass of white wine and gulps it and thinks about how long she should sit there alone. The waiter knows that she is a ballerina who has only just stepped off the stage and he saw her shoulders sink at the sight of the empty chair when she hurried into the café. This combination has made him curious enough to be standing beside the table now, smiling with a mixture of hospitality and intrusion.

'Where is your friend tonight, Mademoiselle?' he asks.

Elise regards the open face of the waiter with its thick, expressive moustache.

'I don't know, Monsieur,' she replies, taking another sip of wine.

'I hope he isn't sick,' the waiter offers. At this, Elise feels something lurch inside her. No, no. She imagines Etienne writhing in agony, his beautiful chest torn open and blood gushing onto his lonely bed and—

'No, I don't think he is unwell,' Elise says calmly.

'Well, the rain, Mademoiselle. It often makes for a slow journey.'

'Yes, perhaps,' she agrees, noticing for the first time that there is indeed a storm this evening and that she is soaking wet. She squelches her feet inside their boots.

'How was the performance?' he asks.

'Excuse me?'

'Tonight, Mademoiselle?'

'Oh yes, yes. It was fine, thank you. A lovely audience. Quite exuberant!' Elise answers, even managing a coquettish giggle as she drains her glass of wine.

'Another?' the waiter suggests.

Elise detects a sympathetic tone in his voice. She sits up very straight in the shaky café chair and smiles broadly. I am perfectly content to be sitting on my own, partaking of some post-performance wine, she thinks. Of course I am. 'Another would be lovely, Monsieur.'

The waiter leaves her table and returns to the bar. Even though Elise is determined not to watch his routine, she is aware of a rather exaggerated uncorking of the bottle of wine and a flourished pouring of the liquid. Even the lifting of the wineglass from the surface of the bar seems to warrant a large gesture that catches in her peripheral vision. Honestly, she thinks, just give me the drink.

The waiter places her wine in the centre of the table. Elise smiles, picks up the glass and turns towards the window of the café. The waiter makes no attempt to converse with her back and returns to his bar once more.

After almost an hour, Etienne arrives. He walks into the café, shakes the rain off his body like a frisky dog, and rushes over to his lover. They embrace, as always, although Elise pulls away sooner than usual.

'I'm late,' he says.

She nods.

'I was painting,' he explains. 'Wait until you see this one! It's alive. The light is wonderful, the figure, ah, I haven't felt so excited by a canvas for some time.'

'Painting?' she says.

'I lost track of the time. I had been at it since noon and the hours passed without me even realising. But the rain started to come through the windows and I had to close them and it was only then that I felt the ache in my back and checked the clock. I was shocked. I'd been standing for almost ten hours.'

'And you forgot you were meeting me?'

'No. I was painting you, engrossed in you.'

'Your picture. You were engrossed in your picture.'

'Yes.'

The conversation continues with Elise making comments that warrant answers and Etienne not noticing that they are even questions. And he expresses his excitement about venturing to the provinces now that Paris has afforded its final inspiration, statements met with an unnoticed silence from his lover. He chatters on until Elise grows increasingly tense and says she is feeling unwell, and they leave together with a fresh distance between them that only one of them has even recognised.

∽

Elise's rehearsal is going very badly. Madame Zappelli is in a fierce mood, already reducing two of the younger dancers to tears. They are hunched over the *barre*, facing the wall, with quiet tired tears trickling out. It takes a lot to make these girls cry. They become adept at managing acute, uncensored attacks on their dancing and their bodies and most of the time they are able to breathe, smile, and use the criticism to spur them on. Their silent resistance to crumbling is relentless. But, this morning, two of them have failed. Two of them, genuinely trying to be as perfect as possible, were attacked by Madame Zappelli, likened to moronic elephants and roundly humiliated. The first one turned away, started to weep and, like a contagious yawn, the second one began to cry as soon as she saw her friend's tears. Their tiny bodies are slumped now and all they are thinking about is their own hopeless fragility, cursing them-selves for being so fallible.

∾

Later, Elise is in Etienne's studio, recounting the details of the rehearsal. She talks and talks and tells him all of it and how much worse it was after the 'rats' had cried and how so much of her time is spent avoiding this infectious misery that pushes through so many of the dancers every day, irres-pective of their status or experience or age, and how hard she finds it to forever remain silent and sweet. She expresses all this with an impassive detachment until Etienne cannot stand to hear another word, until he throws his palette down and stops listening and walks to her and takes her face in his grubby warm hands and speaks.

'When was the last time you were happy?' he asks. 'It was with me, wasn't it? When you were able to forget all that?'

'The last time I was happy?' she says, stalling for time and astounded at his audacity.

'Yes. When did you last feel joyous?'

'Last night, in fact. On stage.'

She watches his face register this as the arrogance slides away. 'I see.'

'Do you?'

'Yes, in performance you are happy. For the few minutes you are on stage, you might feel something like joy. But the rest of the time you are miserable.' And he has become defiant once more and his expression of certainty is back.

'Well, that is enough.'

'I don't think so. I think we must leave Paris and go to the country where you would no longer have to torture yourself with ballet. I must stop talking about this and begin to organise it properly.' And, with this, he releases her face at last.

The idea is incomprehensible to Elise. He has mentioned these plans before, assuming her compliance, and each time the simplicity of his words was absurd to her. She has never uttered her agreement to a departure from Paris, hoping all along that Etienne's talk was fanciful. The distance between them turns into a massive gulf now and she cannot stand to look at him. Etienne shrugs, picks up his palette and walks away. She remains sitting on the stool in his studio. He leans over to fiddle with some paints.

She feels like hitting him but instead she tries to think about how she can explain everything, angry that she even has to. But she is certain that she needs to clarify her situation so these ridiculous suggestions of retirement will stop pervading their time together.

'Ballet is my world,' she blurts out across the studio. 'It's the reason why I was born. There is nothing else for me to do.'

Etienne puts his palette down and turns around to look at Elise, perched on the stool, leaning forward towards him. A pair of cream kid gloves sit in the darkness of her lap like a second pair of hands as her own are clasped together near her face. He waits.

'Can't you understand that?' Elise continues. 'It's like painting for you. Don't you feel that painting is your *raison d'être*—the force that has made you get out of bed every day for as long as you can remember?'

'Yes,' he says.

'I am a ballerina. If I cannot dance, I may as well be dead. And I think I'm lucky to have been given this purpose. So many people are forever trying to understand what they are meant to do with their lives—'

'I know.'

'—and I have always known. For as long as I can remember, I was Elise the ballerina. How can you shrug at me like it is so incomprehensible? Could you try instead to imagine if you were no longer allowed to paint—if someone said to you, Etienne, painting doesn't exist anymore, you should be doing something else. It's absurd, isn't it?'

'But painting makes me happy,' he says.

Elise shakes her head at him, exhausted. 'Is that all you can say?'

He nods.

'Well, it's not as simple as that for me. I don't have a choice. And, Etienne, I don't want a choice.'

The routine of their relationship takes only days to recover. They have one or two meetings in which tension prevails until a small, simple thing restores their intimacy—a spilt drink in the café late at night, a mutual fumbling to retrieve the glass, a gentle banging together of heads as they lean to the floor. And a look. A laughing look at a lover reaching to the tiles. That's all it takes for the affection to descend again and settle back into their hearts. And so life continues as it should with the controversial issue put aside for the moment. Elise dances. Etienne paints. And they tumble together at the end of each day.

Etienne has abandoned his original idea for the series of ballet pictures and has been working instead on a different group of paintings. Ballerinas, yes. But not lightened or bejewelled or washed in misty light. These ones are different.

He will soon show a completed painting to Elise. He is hoping her response will be more favourable than the assault she made on his first ballet picture. After she left the studio that day, he shredded the canvas, hacked through its delicacy with his sharpest palette knife.

He is hoping that the new painting will startle her, wake her up perhaps, make her visible to herself. Maybe even change her mind.

It's a very large canvas, resting on two separate easels that have been pushed together for this moment. It depicts a dark dance studio, clearly recognisable as one of the smaller ones in the Opéra house. There is a door ajar in a corner through which a stream of light pours in a bright diagonal strip across the wooden floor. A tin watering can is next to the doorframe, an accurate rendition of those the dancers use to sprinkle the floorboards with moisture. Most of the canvas is covered by a single figure—a ballerina bending over, adjusting her stocking perhaps, her face looking up towards the open door. The weight of her skirt seems to be pulling her down; the thin ribbon around her neck has come undone; one of her shoes is visibly scuffed; her arms are thin and hanging. She is not smiling.

Elise stands in front of the picture. Etienne is beside her, watching her face and waiting for the expression to change.

'Etienne, it's—I don't know—it's so sad.'

'Yes,' he says.

And she sinks her face into his neck and sobs.

~

Etienne Robert strides into the Halévy colour shop and walks directly to Blanche with his suggestion.

'I would like to exchange one of my recent paintings for the blue panel in the window,' he says.

'The angel painting?'

'Yes. The display has been in place for months now. Were you planning to leave it for much longer?'

'No, no. You're right. It's time for something new.'

'Did you want to keep the panel then?'

'Definitely not. It's served its purpose,' Blanche says.

'So you'll exchange it?'

'Certainly. If you want it, you can have it.'

'Thank you, Madame,' Etienne says with a little bow. 'And I'll also take a tube of your synthetic ultramarine.'

~

Etienne is scrutinising the panel painting. He doesn't have a clear tabletop in his studio so he is sitting on the floor with the picture in front of him and an art treatise pushed open near his right knee. On his left side, there's a glass of red wine. The wine is just beyond his reach and he stretches out towards it, takes a sip and returns it to its place on the floor where its dark fluid is safely away from the angels.

He is beginning to plan his restoration. While he has never before attempted such a process, he is determined about this; he wants the artwork to delight Elise with its rejuvenated beauty.

Etienne scans the ultramarine surface, noting the small lacunae across the sky. He'll overpaint those sections later with a stippling precision. If he's careful, the new pigment will blend seamlessly into the older paintwork, disguising the current blemishes in the blue.

The curve in the wood is quite pronounced. If I leave that alone, he thinks, it will bend itself into a timber tube one day. It must be flattened, he decides. He opens his treatise to the section called 'Cradles for Panel Paintings'.

Later, he will follow the instructions for attaching a wooden framework to the back of a painting to stop its warping curl. He will fix a grid of mahogany strips to the reverse of the panel, making sure that the new addition is able to guide the painting's future movements.

In attaching the cradle, Etienne will think that he is making the panel stronger, ensuring its longevity, supporting it. He does not appreciate the pull of nature. He does not realise that his cradle will damage the painting further, that his intended support will only tug at the wood in a different way.

He picks up the panel now and turns it over. There's an unusual backing paper on the reverse. He peers at it. Frantic fingertips are faintly visible in one section, as though someone has tried to flatten the wrinkling material after it contracted with the application of wet adhesive. Along its edge, the cream paper is already lifting off the wood. Etienne pinches one crisp corner and it tears. He pinches another corner and then begins to peel the sheet away. He wants the panel to be pristine for Elise; he wants it rid of tattered imperfections.

He removes the backing paper in a single, slow shedding.

'Caterina' appears in his studio. Etienne sees the name, notes the childish handwriting. A precocious painter of careful wings, he thinks. How lovely.

He is holding the layer of discarded paper, feeling its old fibres on his fingers. And now he sees what had been stuck on the reverse of the panel: a letter with its words turned down to face the wood. *My beloved STS*, he reads. *I am giving you this painting on the occasion of your wedding… your move to France with Emmeline completes the rupture of our friendship… my heart is irreparable… Think of me, STS, think of me when you observe these cherubs—matching beings flying through a perfect sky…*

Around Etienne, the panel's history is intruding into his plans.

He scrunches up the letter and throws it into a wastepaper basket. And he flips over the panel painting. Angels visible, signature concealed.

A fortnight later, Elise leaves Etienne's studio with the newly restored blue painting placed carefully on top of all the other objects in her tapestry bag. She has not fastened it shut, believing that the angels inside the bag might need to breathe. She recognises her own silliness. She's like a little girl who is infuriated because her doll has been shoved inside a suitcase head first or sat upon by a cumbersome adult. She holds the bag by her side and lets it gently rock as she walks.

Elise thinks about her love as she descends the hill from his studio. She passes La Porte Chinoise—the busy art dealer specialising in objects from the Orient. She drags her hand through the falling water of a fountain and smiles briefly at three old men playing cards on a makeshift table at the edge of the Boulevard. A sparrow flock scatters in front of her as she walks towards home.

Etienne wants to elope. He wants her to run away from the Opéra and escape with him to the country. He will work there, painting pictures that will appear to spill from the edge of their frames. Canvases covered in weather, that's what he wants to create. Yes, this is Etienne's plan. And Elise? Elise can be happy also. With her great love consuming her and the simple beauty of the country. And maybe a child too one day.

He'd planned their rendezvous well. They met, went for a brief walk through the Jardin de Tuileries that was only slightly spoilt by a cascade of chestnuts landing unexpectedly on Etienne's head, then they returned to his studio where the gift of the panel was presented and received by Elise with unquestionable delight. Then, as she sat with the painting on her lap, Etienne knelt on the floor and proposed. With absolute sincerity, he proposed: marriage, her retirement and a new, replenishing life.

Elise reaches the family shop now and steers herself and her rocking bag through the stock. Her parents are attending to a customer and Elise makes it to her bed without any interaction. She sits down, lifts the panel onto the bedspread and pulls a small card out of her pocket. Etienne gave her this note: after the panel, before the proposal.

My darling, she reads. *Thank you for changing the way I see and for letting me paint you. You must know that I would rather paint the woman I love than a simple angel. There are so many of those already, and here are two for you. Two happy creatures with no cares in the world . . . All my love, eternally, Etienne.*

She will tuck this card into the frame of her dressing-room mirror at the Opéra where it will stay wedged beside the looking glass until its corners yellow and curl. One day, she might even accidentally dust it with some face powder as she leans towards her reflection.

Elise turns to the panel, resting in the middle of her bed. The angels seem so content that she feels uncomfortable in their presence. It's as though she is watching a courting couple and intruding on their intimacy. She turns away from the painting and begins to organise her belongings, filling her bag with stockings and greasepaint and a large grey shawl to drape over her shoulders as she waits in the wings.

Once her bag is packed, she sits still with the painting for several minutes: Elise and the angels, side by side on her bed. She is growing accustomed to them, seeing their happiness as something lovely, soothing even. This painting will be my talisman, she decides. No matter where I go, I will take it with me and I will never forget you, my beloved Etienne.

She kneels down, pushes the panel under her bed and straightens the hem of the bedspread along the floor to ensure the edge of the painting is concealed.

She leaves through the shop and begins her journey to the Opéra. She is due to meet M Malikas there before the performance. He has a question to ask her and all the dancers know exactly what it will be: Monsieur Theodoras Malikas, the big man with the big hat, is poised to propose to the dancer. Two in one day. How lucky can a woman be?

Elise is thinking only of marriage as she walks down the Boulevard des Capucines. She is breathing very deeply and deliberately, watching the leaves of the plane trees moving with a breeze not felt below. The sun covers her with splotches of warmth as she paces along the footpath, gulping the air into her lungs in the way she does when she is dressing, in the moment just before her bodice is finally tightened for the day.

Just smile, she thinks to herself, just smile.

7

The panel was burrowed with the threads of sneaky journeys. I imagined the woodworm larvae waiting inside the poplar before it was transformed. Maybe they even felt the swill of Caterina's chalky ground paint as she swept it across the grain: larvae languishing under layers of white gesso that hardened together like an ivory tray. Trapped. Then the worms grew, burrowed around the wood and nuzzled through the picture surface, their tiny exit holes like pinpricks dotted across the paint. Later, they died, either from natural causes or the toxic vapours of previous conservation. They left burrows like lifelines, mapping through the layers.

The paint had peeled and flaked away from the panel. The behaviour of the support—the curve in the wood, the tug of the cradle, the movements of humidity—made it difficult for the picture surface to remain clinging to the poplar. Some small flakes had fallen off entirely—fragments of blue dotted along the centuries—while other pieces defiantly held on. I had reached the stage where those sections could be repaired, where portions of loose paint could be wholly re-adhered.

Warm gelatine, combined with the pressure from a heated spatula, bonded the layers until the flaking portions were merged into the rest of it once more. The procedure reminded me of a time I cut myself with a cheese grater. A layer of skin was shaved off with one edge of it still attached to my hand. I kept pushing the dead skin back over the section of exposed flesh as though, just by returning it to its rightful place, the skin would bond together and there'd no longer be a wound on my palm.

Remember what I used to claim when you teased me? *I've got a thick skin. Say what you like.* As if I were wearing armour. But there were so many layers over me, smothering me, and not many of them protected. Some were just scabby and hard. Some were pliable, like an old bedsheet, waiting to be scrunched or torn. And some were utterly transparent: sliver-thin glass that could suddenly shatter its smudgy self into the rest of me.

∾

By then, your disinterested attitude had begun to prevail: studied apathy from a person who usually cared so much about everything. It was as though you'd developed a commitment to indifference; I'd find myself talking to you, animated and excited, and you'd be staring back at me like a beige brick wall. It had begun with trivial issues: what we should have for dinner or watch on TV or buy at the supermarket. And it soon extended to almost anything I attempted to discuss. During one conversation, your only utterance was to comment on my excessive use of detail.

You stopped trying to get me to deal with the Rotting Room; you suddenly seemed to accept it as an odd component of our home. You made no attempt to feign interest in my work.

The stillness in you made me batty. I felt like I was running around a statue trying to get a response, as though if I waved my arms about enough or pinched a marble toe, maybe a movement might appear in the stone. It made me think of a status exercise you told me you'd once done in a drama class where the group was instructed to move around the studio in pairs, negotiating the ownership of the space with their bodies. You had decided to stay perfectly still and your partner kept moving, moving, moving, trying to intimidate you with all sorts of posturing. But there you were, standing up straight in the middle of the room, watching her. *He claimed the space and won the game just by remaining unaffected by your presence*, the teacher had said to your partner. Then the whole class received a lecture on the power of passivity.

❧

I worked, day after day, with my newfound focus. Forgetting us and you and where we were inevitably heading.

The two blue pigments on the panel—one, hundreds of years old; the other, less than half that age—had been treated differently. A microscopic cross-section of the previous restoration had shown a dirt layer below the newer paint. The synthetic ultramarine had been applied on an unprepared surface, sealing the ancient grit beneath the sheen of blue. I'd carefully stripped away those nineteenth-century 'repairs' and removed the suddenly exposed old dirt.

After the image layer was cleaned and stabilised, the gaps in colour were very conspicuous: absences of hue in an otherwise smooth expanse of sky.

I mixed some putty as a ground coat for the pending patches and applied it to Caterina's missing portions. Then, with a pointy dental tool, I traced on the thin lines of craquelure to replicate the surface of the painting. It was a strange procedure, copying the aging cracks, but it aided the appearance of image continuity. When investigating a forgery, the false craquelure was often an obvious clue— a lazy scammer would scratch a grid across the surface so unlike the random web that came with genuine age, and, immediately, the newness of the painting would be apparent.

I covered the putty background with a watercolour blue I had mixed to match the original ultramarine pigment. The process was akin to darning with paint. When viewed from a distance, my small brushstrokes would blend with Caterina's sky like careful stitches on a swathe of fabric. Only when examined very closely would the new repair be visible.

At home, there was no repair. Only your sustained apathy, punctuated by bursts of anger or confusion.

One night, you were sobbing. Messy, gulping sobs. We'd been fighting for hours about something I can no longer even recall and we'd collapsed together, exhausted by our failure to understand whatever it was we had both chosen to fervently, desperately articulate. You were clutching at me as though you wanted me to consume you, to stretch out my arms and let you disappear. I remember your face, all twisted and wet, and how you were kneading at me like a small kitten. I couldn't stand it. I got up, walked into the bathroom and shut the door, leaving you discarded on the couch.

Most of the time, when I locked myself in our bathroom, it was because I was doing terrible things to my face. I'd attack a tiny red spot—made enormous in the glare of the downlight— until I'd managed to extract a small portion of skin. You would knock on the door after a few minutes of my suspicious silence. 'I've come to rescue your face,' you'd say.

I'd exit slowly, wishing that I was wearing a paper bag. 'I had to get rid of it.'

'But there was nothing there,' you'd say, laughing.

'And there is now?'

'Yes. There is now.' And you'd take my hands and hit them gently and pull one of your terribly-disappointed-with-you faces.

But that night, I just looked at my skin—a messy blur under tears. I thought about chanting a helpful mantra to the person in the mirror, but I couldn't muster a single word to say. Instead, I started to straighten the objects surrounding the sink. Bottles of aftershave (four different varieties), my perfume, some tubs of cream, a hairbrush. I took the toothpaste out of the plastic cup, wiped the brown goo that had collected on the bottom of the tube. I returned it to the cup with the two toothbrushes—green and purple. Always those colours, always that brand. I wiped the basin with a tissue, straightened the tissue box covered in roaming polar bears and turned the soap over so that the malleable, faded side was hidden.

I opened the door and you were still sitting on the couch. I couldn't return to your side.

'I'm sick of this,' I think I said. 'I'm sick of holding on to the dregs.'

And I grabbed my bag and left the flat. I suppose I expected you to follow me or rush to the door or make some gesture. But there was nothing. Just my footsteps, walking away.

It was only once I was outside, in the street, that I realised I didn't have anywhere particular to go. That used to be your trick—the exit as a finale to an argument. But there I was, standing on the street under a yellow lamp, next to a billboard advertising a push-up bra. A woman brushed past me then with tears streaming down her face. A man trailed a few steps behind, yelling at her, imploring her to slow down and let him explain. He was carrying two jackets and a handbag, bundled up in his arms, as if they'd just made a hasty exit from the pub on the corner. We'd been like that once: shamelessly presenting our small dramas to the world.

I waited for them to pass and decided to walk to work. I dug my hands into my bag, felt the cold metal of the keys and the plastic security pass, and turned towards the Centre. I powered along with the loud night rushing past me.

I'd never gone in to work so late, and I had no idea whether I'd find any of my colleagues in there, becoming cross-eyed as they stared at a segment of fragile paint. But when I arrived, accessed the main door and walked through the foyer, it was soon obvious that the entire building was empty. Air conditioning hums dominated the space, as well as the heavy sharp odour of chemicals. I walked towards the lab, switching on each light as I went, leaving a dot-to-dot trail of fluoros behind me.

I reached my workbench and there it was: Caterina's panel, its treatment advanced and its life already partially revived. One day, Ana Poulos would be arriving to take it home with her. I knew I'd have to warn her about the panel's delicacy and provide some advice for its long-term care. I'd urge her not to direct too much light onto the picture. The colours could fade. Or the light could shine, all squinty, into the eyes of the angels until their frail old bodies were forced to turn away from it entirely.

I sat down in front of the panel. The angels seemed different without any trace of sunlight sneaking in through the windows. The craquelure was invisible across their wings and they were softer. And still they flew.

I was grateful that I'd seen the painting in that way, on that night. I was in love with its ambiguity. Its defiant flight.

I am confessing this to you now, my late night visit, as though it were an illicit affair. But I didn't leave you for a panel painting. There was just a certainty about my feelings for that artwork that clarified our relationship to me, at last. People are defined by those surrounding them and when the reflection you get is a distortion, it might not be recognised as soon as it should be.

The clarity was exhilarating. It reminded me of getting my first pair of glasses when I was a child. I walked out of the optometrist's into the street and saw that the clouds were three dimensional, that even the highest leaves had shadows, details that had never been visible to me before. I remember standing there, jaw dropped, staring in amazement.

I couldn't share my passion with you—you were not interested and I didn't know how. The painting simply provided the inevitable circumstances to expose the ineptitude of us. Once I realised that, all I wanted was to be free of you.

~

When I returned home that night, you were in bed, reading. Your legs were long under the doona, your chest bare, with a play script pressed open at your side. There was a black pen tucked behind your ear that you pulled out from time to time. I'd walked inside, into the bedroom, and sat down on the edge of the bed before you even glanced up from the script. I watched you, reflected in my mirror, as you sucked on the pen.

'I'm just practising my lines,' you said. 'Is that okay?'

Your mouth was gently open, lips relaxed. The skin on your cheeks was a bit red, like a little boy who has been running around. Forehead high and crinkling. That face of yours.

'*He's stopped crying. You have replaced him as it were. The tears of the world are a constant entity*, no, no, um, *a constant quantity*. Yep. *For each one who begins to weep, somewhere else another stops. The same is true of the laugh.* Then I laugh. Ha ha ha,' you practised.

I thought that was a beautiful idea: an emotion cycle.

'What if that didn't happen though?' I asked you. 'What if there wasn't a balance? What would happen if every single human being started to cry simultaneously? There could be an enormous flood!'

You simply shrugged, and continued: '... *all my thoughts, all my feelings, would have been of common things.* Longish pause. *Professional worries! Beauty, grace, truth of the first water, I knew they were all beyond me. So I took ...*'

I noticed the edge of a photograph sneaking out from another on the mirror frame. Just a tiny bent corner was visible. I pulled at it and revealed the image: a photo I'd taken years before at Trinity College in Dublin. A simple shot of a curious object: a tiny porcelain woman whose detachable body parts were slotted together for display. She'd been part of an exhibition of Medical Teaching Equipment from Bygone Eras. I'd liked her because she was as small and quaint as a kitschy ornament, yet she was beautiful. And useful. Her tiny white porcelain head rested on a tiny white porcelain pillow with porcelain lace around the edges resembling a linen doily that could never be ripped. Her removable pregnant belly was a perfect round thing with a small spot of belly button. Her eyes were moulded shut and peaceful, unable to open even when her body was being disassembled. I'd taken her photo as she lay quietly nude in a display case right next to a Victorian bone saw and a medical school lecture timetable from the eighteenth century.

I tucked her back into the mirror, wedged her firmly under the wooden frame so she wouldn't slip down again. Later, I got into bed beside you.

'*Forget all I said. I don't remember exactly what it was, but you may be sure there wasn't a word of truth in it,*' you recited.

Then your voice changed and one of our final conversations began.

'Have you almost finished it? The panel?'

'I've reached the final stages.'

'That's good.'

'Is it?'

'Well, you've just been totally preoccupied, that's all.'

'Oh. Sorry?' I suggested.

'No, no, don't be.'

'I wasn't.'

'Good.'

'Mark?'

'Yep.'

'Do you have any idea how you go on before one of your plays starts? It's all you can talk about.'

'Well, it's exciting. New ideas, new people. At least I get excited about real things. About people.'

'What's that supposed to mean?'

'Well, you're more into objects.'

'Goodnight,' I said. You nasty bastard, I thought.

I spent so much of my time restoring things, trying to reclaim their original beauty. All day I looked at deteriorating objects with their parts exposed like a person with her heart on the outside. I could touch them, make a decision and watch them transform. Done.

But then there was us. I'd thought that I had too much faith in two people together. What was it but too much knowledge? I'd thought that I'd rather not be known at all than known in that way by a person who understood where I hurt. I could've been covered in a suit of steel and you'd have found the faulty seam where a pellet of pain could reach me.

You snored beside me, a little purr coming from your mouth. I watched you sleep, watched the face that I saw more than my own, and tried to love it. I tried to think of the last time I'd felt a tenderness for you that had nothing to do with our history, of a moment when I'd loved you afresh without having to retrieve an older moment to make me feel it.

And I knew: I wasn't interested anymore. I was tired of attempting to reach my affection for that person beside me, pulling it into my mind like a decision to try to feel. I just wanted to roll you over and wallow in the silence.

In the beginning, I'd met you one evening after you'd spent all day painting a theatre set. I'd waited on a street corner, trying to appear unperturbed as people shoved past me into shops. The sun was folding into glary wedges of light around the buildings and I remember glancing down at my opaque tights and wondering about their sudden shine. And then I saw you—a spark of colour in that blurring street. As you walked towards me, your face just opened up. Zing!!!!! it said, with a lot of exclamation. And I felt like shouting. *Look at that*, I wanted to say, pointing at you. The beautiful coloured thing that suddenly filled my world.

A man, splattered in paint. And we'd grabbed each other, squeezed until the muscles in my arms started to hurt. And we'd kissed, kissed until our eyes popped open. And we'd laughed.

The night our relationship finally ended, you had also spent the day painting during the bump-in for *Waiting for Godot*. I waited for you, as I had all those years before, after you'd spent hours covering the walls of a forty-year-old theatre with yet another layer of background black.

When you arrived home, you smelled like last night's stubbies, the ones you find after a party with a couple of shrivelled cigarette butts floating in the warm leftover beer. You were tired and your clothes, of course, were streaked with paint.

It was so efficient: an awful, pragmatic conversation. I think you began to cry, but I cannot be sure because I was looking determinedly at a cushion I was hugging on my lap. It took a few minutes, literally, for you to pack up your things. I assisted by making piles of CDs, sorting toiletries.

'You could've bloody waited until my show was over,' you said as you left.

I had to stop myself from laughing at you then: your show will never be fucking over, I thought.

I cannot stand to remember that moment now. How I danced around the living room, moved my pillows into the middle of the bed, exultant.

8

BONEGILLA MIGRANT RECEPTION CENTRE, ALBURY–WODONGA, VICTORIA, 1954

'all I want in front of my window
is a sheet immersed in bluing
spread there like the sea.'

GEORGE SEFERIS, *Five Poems by Mr S. Thalassinos*, 1931

Dimitra Spyrakos is lying on a small cot bed in a camp in the country. She arrived here last night with her husband, Andreas, and their three tired children. It was well past midnight when their bus pulled up at the office and the little ones were already asleep. So, Ari, their baby boy, and Eleni, their youngest girl, were dopily hoisted onto a parental shoulder throughout the registration process. Anastasia, the eldest by only eighteen months, stood quietly awake beside them.

'Block 5, Hut 5,' the family was told in slow, gentle English. A young woman wearing a navy frock speckled with white flowers led them to their lodgings. The Block 5-ers walked across the camp in the darkness, many of them staring only at the sweep of the woman's hair or the flow of her skirt as she strode along; the sole light coming from an enormous torch that she held out in front of her, slicing the way.

They arrived in the dark and fell asleep quickly.

And now Dimitra Spyrakos has woken up. With her eyes jammed shut, she is listening to a stream of names booming from the camp's PA system: '. . . Luigi Cosimmo. Carlos Cosimmo. George Papadopoulos. Heneik Rokowski. Jan Sillins. Hans Verloop . . .' And a jumble of other words in English, firm and demanding.

Dimitra holds her head away from the pillow as though this small upward tilt will place her even closer to the sound. When the announcement finishes, she relaxes her neck and flops her head back down into the straw. To her left is Andreas. To her right is Ari in a cot and, beyond him, the two girls. Beyond them, several more beds full of strangers.

Dimitra sits up. She can feel that the sun has already landed on the corrugated iron wall behind her and she wriggles towards the foot of the bed to get a bit further away from the pressing heat. Her face scrunches as she notices that the legs of Ari's cot are sitting in four tin cans filled with water. An old tomato label still clings to one of the cans. Later, the family will discover that this strange set-up is a way to keep the ants from crawling up the cot legs and across the baby, an innovation left over from the hut's previous occupants. But for the next week, at least, they will frown in confusion at the cot-leg cans until Anastasia looks closely inside them and sees a black film of ants floating on the top of the water.

Dimitra can hear Ari making noises as he stirs. She sighs, kneeling up on her bed to see into the cot. She shakes her head at the sight of him with his arms flailing about and his face still that terrible pale green. Before the voyage, Dimitra would never have believed that a human being could turn such a colour—the colour of sea froth in the shade. But here he is, her baby son. Sick. Sick. Sick.

They all felt ill on the boat at one time or another; they expected that. But no one anticipated the sickness that would overcome the youngest member of the family. His wobbly walking was funny to start with: those chubby brown legs tottering across the boat deck, resembling a mini drunk man. But then one morning he couldn't stand up at all. Dimitra went to wake him and put her hand on his forehead, sticky with wayward hair, and felt the heat of his fever dart up her arm like a shock. She got him out of bed and propped him up against the bunk. She leant down with a bright, animated face and held him under his arms.

'Stand up, Ari,' she said. 'Come on, *pethaki mou*, wake up.'

She let go for a moment and he flopped and collapsed into her hands, groaning. Dimitra scooped him up then, held him tightly against her, patted his small damp head and began to feel a churning panic. She put Ari back into bed with the scratchy blue blanket very loose around his chest and went off to find the ship's doctor: an overworked octogenarian who rushed through the cabins like a whistling sea-wind. Dimitra caught the doctor, explained her problem and gave him directions. The old man touched her gently on the shoulder as he turned to find the child. Soon after, Dimitra reached Andreas and their girls in the breakfast mess hall near the bow of the boat.

'Mana!' the girls squealed when they saw her coming towards their table.

'Hello,' Dimitra said, leaning in to whisper to Andreas. 'Ari is sick. He has a fever.' Andreas stood up as Dimitra turned to her two daughters.

'Eleni and Ana, will you stay here for a while? Papa and I have to go for a walk.' Dimitra looked closely at her girls. They had messy plaits hanging down on both sides of their faces.

'When did you do those plaits?' she asked them.

'Just then,' said Anastasia.

'Well,' said Dimitra, squatting down beside her daughters. 'Why don't you take them out and start again and by the time we get back, you should be finished.'

'Okay,' said Eleni, pulling the strings from the ends of her hair.

'Is something wrong?' asked Anastasia.

'No, no,' said Dimitra, tugging at her daughter's plaits. 'We'll be back soon.'

Andreas and his wife turned away from the girls and hurried back towards their cabin. They pulled each other through the people in the corridors, their arms and fingers tightly together.

'It's just a bout of seasickness,' they were told.

But that was days ago, just before the ship docked at Port Melbourne, and still Ari is feverish. Once again, Dimitra is going to find a doctor.

She stands up and walks towards the hut door, passing the family's two unopened suitcases sitting at the foot of her bed. They all had to sleep in their clothes last night because it was too dark to find anything else and now, for the first time, Dimitra is able to properly see the hut she has already been in for hours. This feeling reminds her of the time she went to visit an old friend in Thessaloniki. She travelled for a day to get there and when she finally arrived, the city had already settled into its night. Dimitra had gone to sleep in her friend's home feeling frustrated, eager for the sun to rise so she could see her new surroundings. When she awoke, the vivid city overwhelmed her and she spent the morning walking down streets she had travelled through the night before, only this time she was able to see them.

Dimitra stands at the door of the hut with her family stirring behind her in their beds. She lifts the squeaky latch near the handle, opens it and is stunned as the clammy air slaps her face. Directly opposite—beyond several feet of pale ground—is another row of corrugated iron huts shining like thermometer juice in the hot morning sun.

An opportunity to unpack comes in between designated meal times and endless administrative tasks. Andreas and Dimitra are alone together in Hut 5/5 looking at their two unopened suitcases.

'I'm going to unpack,' she says.

'Why?' asks Andreas. 'Why do you want to unpack?'

'Why not? We have these two shelves to use.'

'No.'

'What?'

'No. Let's leave our suitcases full. We won't be here for long.'

'I don't know about that, Andreas,' says Dimitra gently.

'No. We are only here for registration, for a couple of days. Then I'll be allocated work and we'll leave. To go to the city.'

Dimitra nods.

'That's what they said,' Andreas continues. 'That's what they told us.'

'I know,' Dimitra says, thinking of the people who visited their village months ago. There was a contingent of six officials, travelling throughout Greece to promote migration to Australia. Government sponsored and seemingly straight-forward, the men in suits made the whole process sound so appealing. They showed grainy films of Australia: beaches, neat suburban streets, productive groups of workers on the Snowy River Hydro-Electric Scheme. Dimitra and Andreas agreed to migrate. They committed to two years in Australia with the promise that they were leaving a place of hardship for a place where they were needed. Those officials generated such intense optimism that the Spyrakos family boarded the ship in Athens feeling as though they were precious seeds about to be planted and nurtured in a new, fertile environ-ment. Andreas even scooped some soil into a jar before the journey—just a small pile of dirt—as a reminder of the futility of their recent farming attempts, and the land that they were leaving. They carried the names and addresses of other people who knew other people who had already made the journey, and they left.

'But, Andreas,' Dimitra says. 'I spoke to a woman this morning who has been living here for over six months.'

Andreas says nothing.

'I'm not going to live out of a suitcase for six months,' she continues.

'We'll see,' Andreas says. And he leaves the hut without waiting for another word from his wife.

Dimitra bends down and lifts the first suitcase up onto the bed. Item by item, she removes their belongings until a pile of clothes forms on the thin wooden shelf between the beds. As a concession to her husband's reluctance, she does not empty the suitcases entirely. Instead she leaves just one thing inside one case: an old panel painting—very fragile and blue—which she has treasured since the death of her beloved grand-mère almost twenty years ago. Dimitra makes a promise now that she will not remove it until they have a new home, until they are settled somewhere as a family in this borderless country at the end of the world. She hardly looks at the picture even though she longs to have a peep at those angels. No, she thinks, it's not time to release them. Her grandmother's old painting is left in the suitcase which is pushed along the floorboards beneath her bed.

∾

The next day, Dimitra is sitting on the bed against one wall of Hut 5/5. A pamphlet she was recently given is open on her lap. It's smaller than a book, thinner than a magazine, with a busy, bright cover blaring with words—*Soyez les Bienvenus! Willkommen! Witamy! Welcome!*—but no Greek. She scans the pages for any word she understands, searching across the faint lines of print for even the smallest piece of familiarity. There are a few words she does recognise, words that jump away from the rest like an odd patch of colour in a jigsaw puzzle: *hello ... breakfast ... lunch ... dinner ... children ... help.*

Dimitra can talk though, talk and talk with the Australians working at Bonegilla. Yesterday, a lady in the kitchen told her about a birthday cake she was making for a child in Block 6. The lady discussed the ingredients with Dimitra and told her she was going to cover the pale yellow sponge cake in pale pink icing. Dimitra suggested she use some wildflowers as decoration. The lady liked the idea and thanked her. It was a small interchange but it is those conversations that give Dimitra hope for something more.

Later today she will go to an English lesson in the Activities Room. If there were three classes per day, Dimitra would probably attend them all. There were English lessons on board the ship, five times a week for the duration of the journey, and she didn't miss a single one. She even slotted lists of new vocabulary into the frame of a small mirror in their cabin to help her memory. During the Crossing of the Equator Celebrations, Dimitra Spyrakos was singled out by the ship's captain and congratulated for her dedication. She was standing on the deck with her family, all of them wearing tissue-paper party hats, when the Greek captain told everyone that there was one passenger who had shown a particularly impressive commitment to learning English. Dimitra remembers looking down at Eleni and Anastasia when he said this and seeing their bright faces grinning up at her with pride. Later, Andreas teased his wife. 'A new language will mean you can talk even more,' he said with a laugh.

This morning, Andreas is playing soccer. The Bonegilla team recently won the inaugural local competition against men from all over the district; it was big news and one of the first things that the Spyrakos family heard about when they arrived. After finishing some mandatory tasks—alien registration, employment registration, tuberculosis screening—Andreas is able to take part in leisure activities for the first time. Indeed, there is little else to do while he is waiting to be allocated work. Anastasia and Eleni are at school. And Dimitra is alone, thinking of them all.

Are the girls sitting next to each other on wobbly chairs? Is Andreas doing tricks with the football? Are they happy? Are they yearning for home? Have they made friends with an Italian? A Maltese? A Spaniard? A Finn? Are they scared? Will Anastasia and Eleni learn English faster than their parents? Are all of them feeling this hot?

But pushing through all other thoughts—of language, of home, of her girls, of her husband—there is Ari, her sick baby in the Bonegilla Hospital Children's Ward. He has malaria and the doctors at the hospital are appalled that his condition was not recognised on the ship. Yesterday, when Dimitra was told about this, she found herself defending the old doctor who had attended Ari during the voyage.

'The conditions on board were horrendous,' she explained to a Greek woman working as a nurse. 'It was good that he had time to see Ari at all given the number of people who needed his attention.'

'I understand,' she said. 'But malaria is a very serious condition and the sooner it's detected, the better. We are now treating a child who is far sicker than necessary.'

Far sicker than necessary. How could any level of sickness in her son be necessary? How could a fever and the horrible shaking of his body be necessary? Just the thought of him— being fed quinine, sitting up and crying in an ice water bath—makes Dimitra want to weep. If only they hadn't disembarked in the tropics; if only the mosquito had bitten her instead of him; if only she had covered his skin.

There are sixteen people living in Block 5, Hut 5. That's three families, unrelated, together in the one hot space. It could be worse; at least they have not been separated. On the ship, they heard stories about families being pulled apart: men in one building, women and children in another, separated by hundreds of feet of dusty ground and the constant gaze of the staff. Far better to be crammed in with strangers and their loved ones than to be crammed in only with strangers. Remaining close to their family seems like the most important thing imaginable.

The 5/5 inhabitants have made this hut as cosy as they can. Against the walls, they have tucked blankets into the gaps between the sheets of hard hot tin. A bit of insulation from the summer outside, they hope. And from the low, slanting roof, there are other blankets hanging down, tenuously partitioning the families. The curtains of grey wool are attached to the roof beams with nails requested from the supply store: two nails on the two top corners. The blankets aren't that big, however, and the legs of strangers—moving in bare feet or boots—can still be seen below the bottom edges. And their voices float through the hut as freely as flies, the languages merging into a mess of noise. Yesterday, Anastasia Spyrakos stood very close to one of the blanket partitions and giggled at the sounds of the Italian family on the other side. They were fighting over something, she thought, and their words were going up and down and round in circles very, very fast. Andreas noticed his daughter's amusement and scolded her.

'The Italian voice isn't funny, Anastasia,' he said, straightening the wall of grey wool. She apologised to him and ran outside.

This morning, the blankets in the hut are perfectly still. They are hanging as lank as greasy ponytails, heavy and dark.

The PA announcements wake the Block 5-ers every morning; the list of names of those who have been allocated work is an agonising alarm clock. Today, like the previous days, Dimitra and Andreas hold hands as they listen to the announcement. They are lying on their backs looking up at the shadowy, cobwebbed ceiling, each with an arm stretched into the space between their beds.

The list ends. Once again, Andreas has not been summoned and once again he slowly pulls his hand away from Dimitra's and rolls to the furthest edge of his bed. Neither of them speaks.

Dimitra watches him for a moment, watches his gorgeous big back in that tiny bed and wants to reach across and touch it. But she leaves him alone and gets up to organise their children, passing Ari's empty cot as she moves towards her daughters' beds.

There is a special activity for the children today. Queen Elizabeth is visiting the area in a fortnight's time and the local council has chosen the Bonegilla school to make some decorative banners for her arrival at Benalla train station.

Miss Whelan is standing in front of her class, clutching her hands together and smiling a smile so wide that it appears to extend beyond her cheeks. There is a row of pictures behind her on the blackboard. The first one is a coronation portrait of the Queen that Miss Whelan tore from a commemorative edition of the *Australian Women's Weekly*. Queen Elizabeth is wearing gown and crown, the first voluminous and lemon, the second huge, glistening and perfectly straight. Next to this is a small photograph of the Benalla train station. In a few moments, Miss Whelan will pull this off the blackboard and pass it around the class so each child can get a closer look. Finally, there is a large book entitled *Native*

Rock Art, pressed open and resting on the chalk ledge, full of close-up photographs of Aboriginal cave paintings.

Mr Wiltshire, Bonegilla's Recreation Officer, is kneeling down at the side of the classroom lifting rolls of calico from a large wooden crate. Miss Whelan struggles to remain focused on the children as she explains the details of their task. Instead, her gaze keeps sneaking across to the abundance of materials being delivered by Mr Wiltshire. For a classroom teacher who is instructed never to waste a stump of chalk, who rations out old documents from the camp's administration offices with one blank side for the children to use, who is constantly attempting to be innovative with gum leaves, these rolls of fabric and the paints that are toppling onto the floor beside them are a truly exhilarating vision.

'Any questions?' Miss Whelan finishes.

'Can we go to the station to see the Queen?' a boy asks.

'No, Gino, you won't be able to go,' Miss Whelan smiles. 'But Queen Elizabeth will think about the new Australians when she sees your banners, and being thought about by the Queen is almost as good as getting to see her.'

With this, the painting starts in earnest. The tables are shifted to form long rows and a length of material is shaken out along each one. Miss Whelan moves down the end of the rows, catching the calico and cutting it off with an enormous pair of sewing scissors. Mr Wiltshire moves along the other end with a less impressive set of pinking shears. Forty-two children scurry around between the tables.

Ana and Eleni Spyrakos stand quietly together as everything reorganises itself around them.

Once the room is striped with fabric, each child is allocated a group, which is then allocated a portion of banner to decorate. Mr Wiltshire distributes the acrylic paints before leaving the classroom to coordinate a women's sewing group in Block 17.

Miss Whelan spends the next couple of hours guiding her class through the basics of Aboriginal art imitation. She lets them consult *Native Rock Art* for inspiration and whispers encouraging suggestions in the ears of the more tentative children. 'It's very easy,' she says. 'Lots of dots and snakes. Just dots and snakes. And maybe some of you could even try a big lizard!'

Eventually, a Dutch child named Anneli Hupps is deemed to be the best Aboriginal artist in the class.

'Dimitra Spyrakos,' the PA booms this morning.

Andreas squeezes her hand. She turns to look at him, confused.

'Me,' she says. 'I have been assigned work?'

'Yes.'

'Me.'

'It's okay,' says Andreas. 'You'd better go and report in.'

'Of course. Of course.'

And so Dimitra gets out of bed and begins to pull on her clothes as Andreas lies silently watching her.

'It's okay,' he says to her again as she leaves the hut. 'Come back and tell me what you have to do. I won't be going anywhere.'

Two hours later, Dimitra is standing in the stinking hot Block 5 kitchen, helping to prepare lunch for two hundred people. She is to work in this kitchen for four hours each day and will be earning the family's first lot of Australian pounds.

Lunch is mutton stew—eighteen pots of it. She peers into one of them, bubbling on the stove, and marvels at the transformation of the small pieces of carrot she chopped up earlier. Already the carrot orange has faded and the pieces of vegetable can hardly be distinguished from everything else that is floating around in the cloudy liquid. There are potato pieces and fat and a few chunks of stringy meat boiling blandly together with her carrots. Dimitra stops herself from thinking about their food at home, the familiarity and the freshness of what she has consumed since her childhood. Of all the things to yearn for, she is not going to allow herself to yearn for an olive.

She arranges slices of white bread like squares of blank cardboard fanned across a large tin platter. She is grateful for this work and the wages and for the fact that it fills in some time. But she wishes that Andreas was the one with employment.

When he arrives for lunch in half an hour, Dimitra will have thought of something reassuring to say to him. Something about patience, perhaps. Or hope. Something that makes him understand that her work here is only temporary and that the real thing they are waiting for is a job for him. She will say these things in the careful way she has perfected over eleven years of marriage: with that particular mix of love and expectation that generates not an inkling of pressure.

With the reassurance that comes from perfect timing, the Spyrakos family is woken the following day by the announcement of a work allocation for Andreas.

Moments later, there is disappointment. The job is just five days of grape picking in the nearby town of Berry. Six men have been selected to make the journey to the vineyard where they will live and work until the end of the week. Andreas has decided that this job is worse than none at all.

'Almost three weeks I've waited. And for what?' he says to Dimitra.

'I know, I know. But it's something, isn't it?'

'Hardly.'

'No, it's something. It's a start.'

'I am beginning to wonder why we are here,' he says. 'If there isn't work for me, there's no reason for us to be here.'

'Please don't say that.'

'We need money. Real money. I have to send some home as soon as possible. How can I do that with five days of wages?'

'There'll be more.'

'And with you working, the children will be alone too much.'

'It'll be okay. The girls are at school for most of the day. And Ari is still in hospital.'

'And what if he doesn't improve, Dimitra? We shouldn't be separated now. What if Ari gets worse and I'm not here when he dies?'

Dimitra glares at her husband, appalled.

'Well?' he insists.

'Don't you dare say that,' she says. 'Our baby is not going to die.' And she bursts into tears.

She cries and turns from Andreas. He tries to touch her and she flicks him away. All she wants is to sob, to feel the tears wash over her face and cover the things that have just been said. *Our baby. Die.* Exactly what Dimitra has refused to say until now. Just the mention of Ari's death has made the idea more feasible. Why can words do this—make an idea real? Why did he have to say that? Why did she?

'Ari will recover,' Dimitra says slowly. And she sighs, messily wipes her eyes. 'You'll go to that place to pick grapes and when you get back, Ari will be well.'

'I'm sorry,' Andreas says, putting his arms around his wife. 'I'm so sorry.'

Dimitra relaxes into him, breathes him in, smothers herself into the darkness of his body and holds on to him as hard as she can.

She looks up for a moment. 'Remember the children quota?'

'Yes.'

'Well, we didn't fight to change the maximum to three children only to lose one after the journey, did we?'

'No,' smiles Andreas. 'Definitely not.'

One of their children is asleep in a small hospital bed. The other two are down at the river that pushes along the edge of the sprawling Bonegilla camp site.

Anastasia Spyrakos is sitting on the bank. The dust between her toes is pale and tickly, reminding her of shaken pepper as it falls around her wiggling feet. She is watching Eleni in the river in the same way she used to do at home when people would swim in the sea and squeal at each other across the turquoise water. Anastasia would always watch from the beach, just at the point where the dry sand compacted into wet.

She has never liked being in the water; there is something about the feel of it all over and around her that makes her confused. She can't push her body through it. Instead, each time she has been submerged, she has wanted to stay absolutely still until it felt as though there was no difference between the water and herself, as though it were possible for her to just dissolve into it like a tablet. Dimitra used to grab on to her legs, make them kick, physically try to adjust the instinct in her eldest daughter to float and disappear. But it was no use. Anastasia's body would not swim.

Each afternoon when the Bonegilla children are released from school, many of them run down to the river. Some of them aren't wearing shoes and as they run across grass covered in prickly bindies, they squeal but keep running, past the blocks of huts, past the kitchen smells, past the gum trees, all the way down the hill to the dirt of the river bank. Then they peel off their clothes and run into the water in tatty singlets and pants, squealing again at the squish and the rocks beneath their toes.

Swimming here is like swimming in an enormous puddle, Anastasia thinks. There's the brown dirt-filled water, the floating leaves and the way the bank slopes into the river just like the crumbling edges of a pothole on a road. And most importantly of all, the river is contained; she can see where the water stops and where the land begins again on the other side. It's not like sitting on a beach where it's possible to stare and stare at the sea in front of you until you really believe that there isn't an end to it at all. Or like looking out from a ship's deck. She remembers one night during the ship's journey when everyone around her was marvelling at the sunset and trying to find the perfect word for the purply-pinky-orangey colour of the sky. But all Anastasia could look at was the endless sweep of indigo ocean—the wide, terrifying stretch of it—that seemed to her to be a vision of nothing if nothing was even something you could put in a picture.

But this river's not scary, Anastasia thinks. The opposite bank is solid and it's covered in the same trees as this bank with their muted long leaves and layers of soft bark that can be peeled off into strips of crooked velvet.

Dimitra has left the heat of the Block 5 kitchen and arrives at the edge of the river. She sees Anastasia and tiptoes up to her, covers her eyes with her hands and kisses her warm little neck. Ana turns and hugs her mother, delighted that she has come to join her in the sun. They sit together on the sloping bank, with their knees tucked up and their light cotton dresses tucked down between their legs. Dimitra pushes off her sandals and nestles her feet into the dusty ground. Now there are twenty toes tapping the peppery dirt.

'You've got ballerina feet, Ana,' Dimitra says.

'Why?'

'High arches,' explains Dimitra as she puts her hand in the space between her daughter's foot and the ground. 'You could fit a big spider under there.'

Anastasia laughs at her mother. 'Like the one in the shower yesterday?'

'Yes, just like the one in the shower. Maybe even a bit bigger. Maybe that spider's papa.'

'Urgh,' shakes Anastasia.

'My French grand-mère used to show me her arched feet,' says Dimitra. 'She seemed like a normal old lady until she lifted her skirts and showed off the muscles in her legs and the shape of her insteps. I can remember her so well; she had big watery eyes and those wondrous legs and feet.'

'Ballerina feet?'

'Yes.'

'Did she talk about it a lot?' Anastasia asks. 'The ballet and Paris?'

'Oh, sometimes. Pappou talked about it even more than Grand-mère though, I think. He admired the Opéra dancers and he went to all the performances when she was the *étoile*. That's French for the star.'

'I know. You've told me before.'

'Oh, of course,' Dimitra says, gazing out over the busy river. 'Pappou used to talk about how beautiful she was. "Ah, Elise, a shining star," he'd say. "When she agreed to marry me, I was the happiest man in Paris." And after their wedding, he was still her greatest fan, sitting in the stage wings on a chair that had his name written on it. *M Theodoras Malikas.*'

Eleni, splashing through a game of keepings-off in the river, sees her family and waves. She does a somersault in the water and finishes it with her arms up and a big ta-daaaa. Her mother and sister respond with a quick round of applause.

'Grand-mère said something to me once that I have never forgotten,' Dimitra continues. 'I was only young, maybe ten years old, like you. She said, "If you find something that makes sense of your world, you must hold on to it for as long as possible." That's what she said. It's nice, isn't it, *pethi mou*?'

'Yes,' says Anastasia, thinking. 'Did she mean ballet?'

'Yes. For her, it was ballet.'

'And she was sad when she hurt her knee and had to stop dancing?'

'Yes,' Dimitra nods. 'Because she understood what it was like to have something and then to lose it and to feel lost yourself. But she liked Greece, she told me. She said she was happy to move there when she retired even though she missed the Opéra very much. Pappou was always proud of that—his elegant Parisian ballerina who became an elegant Kytheran wife.'

'So...' says Anastasia, turning to look at her mother, 'have you found something?'

Dimitra smiles, looks closely at her daughter's small, serious face, all scrunched up with its thoughts and the sun. 'Yes,' she says. 'Your papa and you—my babies. Being a mother, that's my sense.'

Anastasia nods, accepting the answer. 'Maybe you'll have another baby here.'

'Maybe,' Dimitra smiles.

'An Australian baby,' Ana says. 'A French grandma and an Australian baby. You're lucky, aren't you, Mana?'

Dimitra looks at her eldest daughter and feels an enormous pride. She almost thinks it could be visible, this feeling that's pushing inside her. If someone looked at her now, they might see it making her bigger, filling her up like warm, gentle air.

'Yes, I'm lucky,' Dimitra says.

And both of them look ahead at the splashing-squirming-squealing bodies in the river.

The New Australian monthly bulletin is delivered the following day for the first time since the arrival of the Spyrakos family. It's a small publication for the Bonegilla residents, which includes English language quizzes, a list of docked ships from all over the world and general news announcements. 'Norwegian Ship Disaster' is the biggest headline in this edition.

Dimitra is sitting on her bed with a daughter on either side of her, the three of them reading through *The New Australian* together. Anastasia is holding a pocket dictionary and quickly flicking through it to look up any word they do not understand. She was given the dictionary at school after scoring the highest in a numbers quiz, and already the red cardboard cover is beginning to show the wear of the constant clutch of her hands.

Anastasia, Dimitra and Eleni are reading the front-page news.

The Norwegian passenger ship, the SS *Skaubryn*, caught fire yesterday just hours before its expected arrival at Station

Pier, Port Melbourne. The ship was travelling through Port Phillip Bay at the time of the disaster and is reported to have sunk in less than thirty minutes. Miraculously, not one of the three hundred and sixty people on board was drowned.

The Norwegian crew of the *Skaubryn* handled the emergency well with all on board safely evacuated in life-jackets. Not all passengers were able to fit into lifeboats and many were forced to remain immersed in the water for several hours. The conditions on deck were understandably desperate, with many parents reportedly throwing their children overboard to secure them a place on a lifeboat.

All passengers and crew were eventually rescued from the bay by the Australian authorities. One witness described the scene on land as 'pure chaos. Wet children trying to find their parents, everybody crying, reunions everywhere, people searching for their bags.'

The *Skaubryn*'s cargo of three hundred immigrants, all from non-English speaking Europe and almost half women and children, will arrive at Bonegilla Migrant Reception Centre in the next couple of days. Already the Wodonga Boy Scouts and the local YWCA have begun to coordinate a donation drive to assist in providing replacement clothing and toys for this disaster-struck group of new Australians. It is anticipated that several truckloads of donated goods will be waiting to greet them upon their arrival at Bonegilla.

Margaret Davis of the YWCA commented, 'These poor people have already left so much behind and now for them to lose their scarce belongings, well, it's very sad. We'll be doing all we can to welcome them to their new country.'

The cause of the fire is not yet known.

After almost half an hour, they have managed to decipher the basic details of the article.

'Imagine if that happened to us,' Anastasia says.

Dimitra nods.

'Imagine what would have happened to Ari,' says Anastasia.

Dimitra shakes her head.

'And Eleni,' Ana continues. 'And our bags.'

And Grand-mère's painting, Dimitra thinks, suddenly visualising the small poplar panel at the bottom of the ocean, a worthless piece of flotsam. Grasping seaweed, greedy molluscs, bloated chubby angels.

Eleni hasn't said a word.

Both girls are clinging to their *mana* and Dimitra is thinking quickly, quickly of something she can say to them. It is wonderful that no one died, she thinks. All those passengers will be arriving here soon, she thinks. You can make friends with them, she thinks. The local people are being very kind, she thinks.

'We're okay,' she says, pulling them close. 'We're okay.'

෴

Dimitra would go to the hospital as soon as she got up each morning. Yesterday, she walked straight into the long Children's

Ward with its rows of small white beds, straight to the one assigned to Ari, second from the end on the right.

He wasn't in it. The starched sheets were stretched tightly over the thin flat mattress; the pillow was centred and full.

Dimitra grabbed the steel base of the bed. She thought she might faint, or scream, or both. Where is he? *Where is he?*

And then she heard it.

'Maaanaaaaaa!!!!' Shouted from the door of the ward.

Dimitra turned to see Ari tottering towards her as fast as he could. A smiling nurse stood at the door behind him. Dimitra watched her son coming closer with a blissful look on his face. He was freshly scrubbed, wearing a new shirt and an enormous pair of shorts belted around him with a length of ribbon. His dark curly hair had even been neatly parted.

Dimitra ran towards him and scooped him up.

'He's going to be fine,' the nurse said to Dimitra. 'You can take him to your hut now. But bring him back each day for a check-up.'

And now she is watching all of her children racing around the cramped space of Hut 5/5 like twigs caught up in a whirligig. Ari is giggling, tugging at the hem of Eleni's pale blue dress. His huge brown eyes, framed with long lashes wasted on a boy, have their cheekiness restored. Dimitra can hardly believe it.

'Come here,' she says now. And Ari runs to her and lands on her lap with a happy yelp. She laughs and smothers him in kisses.

'Your papa is going to be back tonight,' she whispers to him. 'Isn't that good?'

Ari nods and plants a big sloppy kiss on her ear.

❧

Sometimes people can't help thinking in opposites. If they're lying in the sunshine, they'll think about a torrential storm and how glad they are not to be lying in one of those. They'll look at a child's joy and be reminded of an adult's cynicism. They'll be leaving a place and they'll be thinking about their arrival.

As Dimitra boards the train departing Bonegilla, she is focused—apart from making sure all three children find a seat and wondering whether the sandwiches she packed for the journey will get squashed inside their suitcase—she is focused on remembering the first day her family stepped onto Australian land and were shunted towards that camp in the country.

When their boat first docked at Fremantle, the Spyrakos family chose to stay on board. While migrants travelling to the eastern coast were permitted to leave the ship temporarily, Dimitra was determined not to risk losing a member of her family so close to their destination. Anastasia was particularly upset with the ruling.

'But we got out at Colombo and Port Said,' she complained.

'Yes, I know we did,' Dimitra said. 'But we may never have another chance to visit those places, so that was different.

We are in Australia now and we must all make it to Melbourne together. What if one of you goes missing here and that's the first thing that happens to us in this country? We lose a child. No good.'

Andreas squeezed Dimitra's hand as she said this. Squeezed her hand and smiled.

'Be patient, Ana,' he said. 'We'll be getting off in a few days.'

But the first thing that did happen to Dimitra in this country wasn't quite what she had anticipated either. Ari was in Dimitra's arms when she wobbled on sea legs down the gangplank behind her husband the day they arrived in Port Melbourne. She tripped, fell down and dropped her son. And that was Dimitra's Australian arrival—almost kissing the ground on her hands and knees while her sick child rolled away from her and came to a stop at the feet of his father. Dimitra acquired two neat grazes that have now turned into the scabs of a schoolkid. In a few years, only two small scars will remain—one on each knee—as a reminder of that moment. She will plonk her children beside her and show them those scars and laugh.

Ari wasn't hurt in the fall. Andreas picked him up and held him in one arm while he reached down with the other to assist Dimitra, who was blushing brighter than he'd ever seen her. Anastasia and Eleni stood by and giggled loudly at the sight of their mother on her knees, while Ari's tired crying added to the chaos. When Dimitra got to her feet,

Andreas leant towards her and gently kissed the colour on her cheeks. She closed her eyes for a second and sighed.

Moments later, the family was moved towards a waiting train with hordes of other arrivals. The British migrants were guided in a different direction, to a coach that would take them to a hostel in the middle of the city.

'I feel like a goat,' Dimitra said to Andreas as they moved with the crowd. 'I wish someone could explain where we're headed.'

'We have to be registered,' Andreas said with more conviction than he felt. 'Just hold on to the girls.'

Dimitra is remembering this arrival as she sits on the departing train. They have been in Australia for almost two months, she realises now, and will see Melbourne for the first time in a matter of hours. She puts her arm around Ari beside her and smiles at his legs sticking out straight, the size of him making the hard train seat seem enormous. Anastasia and Eleni sit opposite each other on the window seats, both of them staring out at the flat dusty paddocks rushing past. Their legs swing with the rhythm of the train, softly kicking each other over and over.

Andreas had returned from the vineyard with some good news. A man he'd met there was about to move to Melbourne to start working at a car factory. Many workers were needed, he told Andreas, and by the end of their time in Berry, both men had arranged a work allocation on the factory floor. They returned to Bonegilla for one day and then left again for the city. Dimitra and the children were to follow, once Andreas had secured a home for them somewhere in Melbourne's north, in the area where the blocks of factories and the neat suburban streets are separated only by the stretch of a wide, thundering road.

Andreas left Bonegilla a fortnight ago and already his family is coming to join him. His last letter to Dimitra was a hurried, excitable mess, as though the time taken just to form the words might delay their arrival even further. *I cannot wait to have you all with me again*, he wrote.

Everything will feel better when they're together, Dimitra knows that. Not normal, but better. She is so anxious to arrive, to see Andreas, to walk inside the house that he has described to her in the matter-of-fact way that a man will often describe a home. Date of completion: 1927. Number of rooms: five. Floor measurements: fifteen squares. It's on a long, broad street lined with elm trees and two of its five rooms will be theirs alone. The other three are shared between two brothers and a newlywed couple, all of whom have been in Australia for just a year. The bride's uncle knows one of Andreas' cousins from Kythera and it was this old connection that enabled him to contact the couple in Melbourne. *They are looking forward to meeting you all*, Andreas wrote.

Dimitra is relieved that there will be people to whom she can freely speak, people who will understand how she can yearn for two places at the same time: one she has grown up with and one she has barely seen. But above all, Dimitra is relieved that they will be reunited with Andreas.

She is tired of being incomplete. She is tired of four of them when there should be five. Ari in hospital, then Andreas gone and Ari out of hospital, then the whole five for only a day, then Andreas gone again. Four. Four. Four.

She is tired of this absence after so much else has been lost: her parents, her grandparents, her older brother in the fighting; their home, their work, almost their hope. So many holes gaping inside her and it is only her family—the solid five of it—that comes close now to filling her up.

It is other people who make us whole, Dimitra thinks. Not the places we live in and definitely not the things we have. So she clings to her son beside her in the way she has been doing since he was released from hospital. Clinging to her son, watching her girls, and thinking of Andreas as the train rushes towards the city.

A couple of days later, Dimitra is alone in their bedroom, unpacking their belongings into clean empty cupboards.

She lifts the last piece of clothing out of their suitcase and uncovers the only thing that has yet to be removed: the work of art that has been resting in the bottom of the case since the moment she packed her things in Kythera.

'Hello Grand-mère and Pappou,' she says to the two round angels in the painting.

She smiles at the cherubs and lightly touches the rich bright blue of their world.

There is a nail on the wall beside their bed, a spot where someone else's something has once hung. She turns the panel over and looks at its back for a space where the nail could fit. The cradle on the painting is a grid of wooden strips, each piece separated by a finger's worth of space. Dimitra lifts the painting towards the wall and carefully hangs it there, letting the nail slot into one of the gaps in the cradle.

She steps back and sits down on the edge of her bed and watches the picture. A piece of ultramarine against a vast white wall. Those creatures flying, free to breathe once more.

And then Dimitra Spyrakos flops backwards onto the bed, her arms outstretched on either side and her face covered in sudden tears, kicking her legs up into the air like a child.

9

I made an appointment to go to the framer's to discuss the long-term display possibilities for the blue panel. I wanted to prepare a file for Ana Poulos that included some information on caring for the picture once its restoration was complete. From what I could understand, she'd previously hung it from a nail, slotting it into one of the many small gaps between the cradle strips that criss-crossed the back of the panel. Obviously, with my removal of the cradle, that was no longer going to be an option.

I sat in the waiting area at the framer's, with several other people nearby. Beside me, an elderly man had a 1920s wedding photograph on his lap, slipped inside a plastic pocket. It looked like the kind of stationery item his grandchild might have extracted from a school folder, with handy holes punched down one side. The photograph was a stylised studio image reminiscent of a retro fashion shoot. The bride was exquisitely groomed with her bobbed hair swept low around her ears and neat, slightly smiling, rosebud lips. She was holding a sheaf of lilies, unusual for a wedding bouquet, I thought. The flowers accentuated the elongated line of her gown, lightly skimming her trim, shapeless figure. Her groom was a perfect vision of old-style dapper: three-piece suit, slicked hair and divine posture. The old man—his liver-spotted hands resting on the edges of the plastic pocket—was quietly snoozing. I saw the band of burnished gold around his finger and his distinctive large ears, and realised that the photo was of him. Then I did the sums and decided that he didn't look a hundred years old.

Opposite me, a neat, petite woman was holding a cream leather album (with *Our Wedding* emblazoned in gold script on its cover), gently moving her ankle in circles as she waited to see the framer. It appeared to be a popular day for wedding photos. The woman glanced intermittently at the finished products displayed on the walls around us. She seemed most interested in a framed photo of a pair of white bridal shoes—one of those popular close-up images that are perhaps meant to capture a sense of individual detail. Those photos always reminded me of evidence from a crime scene: the shoe, the button, the wristwatch, the hand. I imagined what curious body parts were included inside her album—perhaps the nape of her neck through a train of tulle, her pedicured toenails with a garter.

Sitting in that framer's office, I felt so surely single and conceited. I saw those wedding photos and almost scoffed at them. I marvelled at the people there who had chosen to entwine themselves so officially. And I had little comprehension as to why anyone would want to do such a thing.

I had already forgotten the passion of possession that could throb between two people. You were right about that— I was more into objects. Because there I was, thinking only of a small painting on a piece of poplar.

Once you were gone, I set about cleaning out the Rotting Room. It seemed like the correct post-break-up behaviour. A plumber came and inspected the damage. He stepped over all my ruined objects to poke around inside the sodden wardrobe. I watched as his large body crouched down inside it, pressing the wall gingerly with expert fingers. When he retreated, he shook his head at my belongings spread out across the carpet. And he suggested that I invest in some large plastic boxes for waterproofing in the future. I was very embarrassed about that: a professional conservator needing household tips for document storage.

He explained the cause of the problem: the shower seal had disintegrated and each time it was used, water overflowed into the space behind it: the study wardrobe. It had been happening for months, apparently, and could only be repaired by the removal and reinstallation of the shower recess. In addition, the shelving in the wardrobe, and much of the carpet in the study, would need replacing. I was lucky, the plumber told me, that I'd found the water when I had and that it had flowed through gradually, that a lot of the liquid had been absorbed by the contents of the wardrobe. I was lucky, he told me, that the water hadn't built up, rupturing into the study in one great flood.

When he was gone, I wanted only to clean it all up. I went along with the cathartic impetus, pulling three dark green garbage bags from a kitchen drawer. I simply walked into the study and filled them. One after another, the bags gained weight, until my piles of ruined history were shrouded inside plastic.

I carried them to the rubbish room in the basement of the building. I had to make several trips up and down the darkened stairs, releasing each bag into a bin. The residue of the mess remained on the carpet and on my body— determined little particles of pulverised paper. I stood in the emptied room, picking at my clothes like a monkey.

It made me think of the autumn leaves you'd once sent me. Each of them was a different colour and later you'd told me how you'd chosen them, one by one, from underneath a row of plane trees near our flat. I'd opened an envelope, tipped it upside down and watched all those leaves drop out. A small square of red paper floated with them. *Happy autumn, lover. May yours be full of colour*, you'd written on it, in that wonky boyish print. I'd spent a long time looking at those leaves. I held them up to the light to x-ray their skeletons. I stroked their pointy, crinkled edges. I smelled their smell of dirt. I arranged them in a perfect scale of blending colour, from the see-through gold to the oldest waxy burgundy. Then I placed them back inside their envelope, sealed it shut again like a time capsule. But for days I'd found tiny crumbs of leaf still clinging to my clothes.

After disposing of all the garbage bags, I vacuumed the floor of the study and changed my top, exhausted.

It was close to Christmas then and, feeling newly house-proud, I found some old decorations in the back of the pantry: threads of silver tinsel and a few random baubles. I hung the baubles in various places: a doorknob, a sturdy branch on a potted palm, the frame of a dining chair. It took me a bit longer to decide on a home for the tinsel.

In the bedroom, there was a blank wall that had held your mask collection until you'd pulled them down on the night you left. I could recall each of the masks staring out at me in chronological order. There had been a couple from cheap show bags you'd cherished as a boy: pieces of dented plastic superhero with fraying white elastic still attached to the tiny holes next to the eyes. There was a *Phantom of the Opera* mask with smudged stage make-up collected along its edges, straight from your starring role in your high-school production. There was a daggy set of brass tragedy/comedy masks that had been a gift from your parents on your acceptance into drama school. There were cardboard replicas of Edwardian ladies bought from a museum in London, and a porcelain Pierrot face with one glittering golden tear. My favourite had been a wicker Vietnamese clown covered in splashes of green.

All that remained after your departure was a series of nails in formation across the white. I draped the tinsel around the nails until the wall was decorated with crossing threads of silver like the lines that appear on a star chart to reveal a saucepan or the Southern Cross. I remember feeling festive and content, so happy with myself for being alone.

∾

I was getting increasingly anxious about losing Caterina's panel. The idea of it leaving the lab started to feel like another pending break-up.

What's breaking up? The idea that two people together is a thing. Some whole that can be snapped in half. Leaving what? Two new pieces? Two confused fractions like scribbles remaining on a blackboard?

You and I broke apart with a neatness that belied our years of mutual dependence. There was barely a single fibre still pulling between the two new pieces that were formed. You'd taken everything on the night you'd left and we hadn't spoken to each other since. There was no overwrought follow-up. No occasional lapse back into bed. No relentless raking over what could have been different or better or worse. None of that. It was a clean cut, no buts, snapping out of coupledom.

But then, after two neat weeks, you called.

'Hey, it's me.' (*It's me*. Did you know that you're the only person I've ever allowed to say that without going through the game of pretending I didn't know who was speaking? I found it infuriating when *me* became a self-declared label.)

'It's me,' you said again.

I stayed silent on the end of the phone line, waiting.

'It's *Mark*.'

'Oh hi, *hi*,' I said. Like a bitch.

But we got through the phone call, asking each other questions we could easily answer about other people we both knew.

How could we have turned into strangers? It amazed me that people could adjust like that, that entwined human beings could untangle themselves the way that they did, that a person who'd shared every intimacy with you could be slotted back into the mass. And I'd thought it was so *sad*—perhaps the most significant change that had happened to either of us in years was happening to us both but there was no way we were going to be sharing it. I wondered about all those infinitely civilised ex-couples you hear about who share the pain of their break-up, help each other meet new people, adjust seamlessly into a nurturing friendship.

You had something to give me and something to tell me, you said. You wanted to catch up and I conceded, and so we made plans for the following afternoon.

When I walked into the designated café, you were already sitting down, doing 'nonchalance'—chair pushed a bit away from the table, sunglasses on top of your head, one elbow propped near the sugar bowl, the other hand flipping through the pages of a magazine, intent on the flashing pictures, ignoring any arrival noises, nearby conversations or people rubbing past your chair.

I did what I was meant to do; I followed the script. I walked over to the table, pulled out the chair opposite you and sat down.

You looked up with a start. 'Oh, hi!'

I considered saying that it surely wasn't a surprise that I'd arrived, that you must have noticed me, all of that. But I realised with quick relief that if you wanted to feign shock, I no longer needed to point out the absurdity of it. You were wearing a t-shirt I'd always hated: bright orange with a silhouette of Marilyn Monroe on the front, composed of a blurry stars 'n' stripes pattern. How petty, I'd thought. 'Nice t-shirt,' I think I said.

And then you leant over the table and kissed me on the cheek. And the warmth rushed in. I looked at your face, into your eyes, and I tried only to chat, to smile, to not know you like I did. I concentrated on remaining impassive while so much of me wanted to reach towards you, touch you, yell at you or make you cry.

For a long hour we remained committed to staying on the civilised, perfunctory side of conversation. There were countless moments when we could have slid back into intensity, when we could have snapped at each other, delved into things. But we didn't. Later, I wished so much that we had.

You told me that you were going on a holiday, alone. 'Island lolling in Thailand,' you explained. 'And then to Laos for a few days.' You told me you were leaving before Christmas, that you'd got the first flight available after the close of *Waiting for Godot*.

Then you reached to the floor and lifted up a white envelope, delivering it into my hands like a decree. I pulled out the two large photographs inside. Caterina's panel. One 'before' shot. One 'after' shot.

'Mark. When did you—?'

'I got them from the Centre. I asked Gillian for the negatives and I picked these two because I thought you'd like them blown up.'

Once the panel was gone, I would still have access to the material I'd collected during the conservation process—all the charts and x-rays of its layers. But these photos were different; I was touched by what you'd chosen and their careful reproduction on thick photographic paper, resplendent in white borders.

'What did Gillian say?' I asked then.

'Well, I spoke to the other paintings conservator about it initially and she gave me a lecture on intellectual property, pre-empting all sorts of difficulties with me getting access to the material,' you explained, enjoying the fuss.

'Joy,' I laughed.

'Yes. But Gillian was fine. She arranged it very simply and said it was a nice idea.'

'It is,' I said. And I thanked you.

And then you jumped from your chair and hugged me. I pulled away, too quickly.

As we departed, I asked you to send me a postcard from Thailand.

'Of course,' you answered. 'As always.'

That was our last, banal conversation.

When I returned home, I went to wedge the images of Caterina's panel into my mirror frame. But I realised there was no space for anything new. So I began to remove the layers. I prised off the pictures, every one—the Madonna face, the Rothko, the Sistine Chapel, the red-faced Mark, the porcelain lady, the perky Raphael cherubs, the countless cards—and piled them into a plastic bag that I later placed in the bedroom cupboard in the space previously filled by your reeking old suitcase. I cleaned the mirror. I peeled off the wads of tape and Blu-Tack until my fingers were sticking together. I squirted the glass with cleaner and wiped over it several times. Eventually, the mirror was shining. Shining and clear, for the first time in years.

And only then did I lodge the panel pictures into the edge of the glass.

There was one other piece of paper that I returned to the frame, a quotation I'd found and copied: *I think the exhilaration of falling out of love is not sufficiently extolled. The escape from the atmosphere of a stuffy room into the fresh night air with the sky as the limit. The feeling of freedom. Of integrity...* It had seemed so pertinent and profound. For the briefest amount of time.

I had a week off work over Christmas. I relished the time to potter around at home, to nest alone. But I had parties to go to almost every night and family events that always lasted a bit too long, fielding questions about our break-up from countless ill-informed relatives. I thought of you often and envied your decision to avoid the inevitable harassment of the newly single by leaving the country during the festive onslaught. I imagined you transforming into tanned relaxation, as summer showers spoiled my own attempts to do so.

But then, one morning, I went and bought *The Age* and glanced at the headline as I left the shop. *Massive Tsunami*, I read. I clung to the newspaper, resolutely refusing to read it as I walked back to the flat. One foot in front of the other, I made it home.

I looked at the front page. *Thailand. Phi Phi. Wave.* Odd words were clear but I was unable to read the endless columns of text. I couldn't fix on a paragraph, I couldn't choose a starting sentence, I couldn't comprehend a caption. But the images . . .

I felt boneless, emptied, as though there was nothing within to keep me standing. I slumped into the couch cushions. And all I could do was concentrate on breathing. Because anything else seemed suddenly impossible.

I spent two days scouring the Internet for information. I became engrossed in seismic reports, meteorological reports, so foreign to someone more accustomed to conservation reports, research reports. I tried to understand the precise direction of the wave, the magnitude of the earthquake. I wanted to see every chart, graph, statistic.

Tsunamis can make the water at a beach disappear. I discovered this. The tide goes out further than one could ever imagine, leaving desperate fish, flitting and exposed. I read about tourists who ran out to see such fish, peering over to look inside their gaping gills, who ran out to inspect the random tide and ran further towards their own vulnerable exposure. And they stood there, tiny humans in the path of the monumental wave as it returned even faster than the tide had vanished. Surging, engulfing and consuming.

And I read about divers, happily exploring a beautiful place in the ocean—whole clusters of them with heavy, high-tech equipment strapped to their torsos—who just disappeared from the water. After the tsunami passed their patch of paradise and the water was calm once more, there was simply no sight of them, no remnant whatsoever.

And hundreds of fishermen in boats, bobbing benignly in their own trusted sea, who vanished along with every last fibre of their nets and baskets.

And so many roaming, stunned children.

And one person in Kenya. And hundreds of thousands in Sri Lanka. And. And. And I read these things and my body shook. And I tried to imagine you, one Australian man somewhere who wouldn't move off his beach towel to inspect a tide, who didn't dive or fish. I tried only to imagine you within none of those stories.

Your mother rang me. The woman who had never really embraced me. I don't mean literally, of course. As you witnessed, I was the occasional recipient of an air kiss above my ear and a hug that involved one arm draped across my back, the other pushing me away with pressure on my collarbone. But she rang and told me. That was infinitely good of her.

Her son had just died. I was his most significant ex.

She sounded sedated, oddly calm, as though the sentences she was uttering were not coming from her body. I tried to express something suitable to her; I tried to wade through my own shock and somehow speak to a woman who had just lost her child. In the end we were both crying. I made a stupid offer to send her some photos of you.

'I have plenty of photos of my son,' she said.

I apologised. She apologised. We hung up.

I thought about how often various relatives of ours had implied that we should have married. We spent years together, we were old enough, it was an option, but, instead, we parted. The woman who could have been my mother-in-law had called to tell me that the man who could have been my husband had died in a tsunami on an island, eating breakfast at a hotel. Which meant I could have been a widow. But I wasn't a widow. I was merely someone who had left a man who had been killed. There were no archaic labels to define me. No way to grieve that I could understand.

'He went to Thailand to recover from you,' she'd said.

To that truth, I had no reply.

For me, regret had been a poorly ended conversation, an unnecessarily harsh word to someone who may not have deserved it. That was regret I understood. But then, I was consumed by a newer and more terrible kind. I regretted the way I had treated someone in his last months of living.

We should have broken up; that became almost incidental. But I shouldn't have left you, forgotten you, discarded you, in the way that I did. And that regret became the awful core of a very confusing grief. Every day, I'd wake up and the feeling would be there. Pain as heavy as the flu, before I'd even had a chance to move.

Writing this story, writing it to you, is my poor attempt to decipher it. I am able to explain things that I hadn't explained in my haste to be free from a relationship that I recognised was wrong. When we broke up, all I wanted was to be free of you. But, if I'd known—where you'd go and what would happen—I would have been more careful with you. That is all. That is everything.

I retreated further into work and the possibilities of the panel.

10

VENICE, 1478

So Niccolò, the banished apprentice, leaves the Venetian lagoons. Just as the highest floodwaters in thirty-four years surge through the canal maze and devastate his *maestro*'s family. All the precautions that Venice could muster do not control the water's force; it rises beyond expert predictions and drowns whole quarters of the city. A weather pattern somewhere above the Adriatic may have caused the sea to betray its people: an inexplicable twisting pressure that is beyond anyone's understanding. The flood's waves are in a hurry to engulf the terrain. They arrive with a sudden force that splashes and pours through the city and then just drains back into the sea expanse once more.

A girl, thirteen years old, clutching at a notebook crowded with angels, is found in the dirty silt of the subsided waves.

She is close to the San Zaccaria convent: one of many people found bloated and blue nearby. She is covered in plaster from the convent's building site, the powder gathered up into the flood and smeared like paste over the surrounding mile. What remains is a sticky coating of filthy white over two *piazzas*, countless buildings and three slippery wooden bridges. Dregs of plaster float among the debris of the waterways, congealing in gummy threads along the tide lines. The nuns find Caterina, carry her into a small dry corner of the convent and wipe her clean. A young novice recognises her as the girl who often smiled from the opposite side of the forecourt fence.

The nun weeps silently as she tries to wash the matted plaster from Caterina's long dark hair, clots of white sneaking under her fingernails while she works.

～

The twins, Giorgio and Segna, howl and howl when their mama, Isabella, tells them that Caterina is gone. They cry so loudly that something changes in them for good. No longer resembling a pair of carefree *putti*, they know things now. Their faces, pulled into the shape of grief, will take years to settle back into contentment.

Their father takes to his bed, pulls the covers up to his whiskers and shuts his eyes, and their mother, dressed in black, cleans their home with a dazed unwavering determination. The boys are instantly well behaved: they fetch soup for their father and step quietly away from Isabella's broom as it strokes the floor, over and over again.

As grief washes through the family, the workshop beneath their home keeps behaving as a workshop should—maintaining commissions and purchasing materials and functioning within the more manageable realm of commerce. The apprentices take over operations after the flood, guided by their fearful respect for the *maestro* and their gratitude that the premises were spared. They are well trained, of course, and behave as people often do when confronted with the crisis of another; they rise to the occasion, suddenly increasing their own capacity to cope. Now and then, one of the apprentices takes the twins to the market for food: two small boys with their dark heads lowered and a bigger boy between them, pulling through the snaking warren of the city.

Isabella is sweeping the floors of their home, wearing a black skirt that catches clouds of flying dust in its folds. With hard wrists and lifted shoulders, she grips the broom handle like a weapon. Quiet tears fall from her eyes. She is sweeping the floor in stripes—along that wall and down there, across there, back again, up and down. Her head drops as she sweeps and occasionally her tears hit the floorboards, pooling for a moment before sinking slowly into the wood.

Once Isabella has covered every last floorboard with her broom bristles, she decides to clean the few pieces of furniture in the room. She props the broom against the wall and leans over to pick up a small wad of soft brushing feathers.

The dark sleeves of her dress are too long and the cuffs hang low over her hands as she walks towards the decorative *cassone* in the corner. She kneels down in front of it and opens the lid. Yesterday, she emptied its contents but now she has no recollection of doing so. The sight of the blank base startles her and she slumps onto the floor, confused. I must have taken out Caterina's clothes, she thinks. She sits there and tries to pull the memory of this into her mind. She shakes her head, tells herself to think carefully about everything she has done. Later, she will ask Giorgio where Caterina's clothes have gone and he will tell her about the morning they spent folding them together and how she asked him to take them to the workshop and establish whether the workers could use them for their families. *I see*, Isabella will say to her son. *Thank you, Giorgio*, she will say. *Did you forget, Mama?* he will ask her and Isabella will not lie. But now, she does not know and cannot remember and is shutting the emptiness of the chest away from view. She sweeps the feathers over the closed lid, catching several of them in the pointed wooden inlay.

Isabella stands up, determined to clean behind the chest. She drags the *cassone* away from the wall, towards the centre of the room. There is a sudden bang as something behind it falls flat onto the floor. It is a piece of wood.

She drops the feathers and wipes her eyes. With both hands, she wipes and wipes and blinks and blinks until the film of tears is gone and the letters on the wood are perfectly clear.

Caterina, she reads. *Caterina*.

Isabella bends down to lift the panel off the floor, turning it over to reveal a sudden flash of blue. She stares at the painting in her hands and tries to understand what it is that she is looking at.

A panel piece. A panel painting. And they're my boys. Those cherubim. Two angels in the sky. Painted by Caterina. With lapis lazuli. Oh no, lapis lazuli. Niccolò. Niccolò stole it for her. Lapis lazuli. Those wings. She painted the most exquisite wings. And they're flying. Flying. Oh my baby. I must take this away, hide it from the workshop, the guild. Caterina, this is beautiful. I must take it somewhere safe.

'I will take it somewhere safe, Caterina,' she says.

Isabella holds the painting away from her, aware of its fragile layers and the fall of her tears. And with her sad gaze fixed on the ultramarine sheen, she begins to think of all the places it could go.

II

You were listed and labelled in the newspapers. *A twenty-nine-year-old actor from Melbourne. Body still not found.* Your parents were mentioned too. *Their only child.*

Your headshot was always there among the line of grainy victim photos: a perfect studio photograph amid several others cropped more frantically from family snaps or a video still. One victim was always pictured at the moment she was blowing out birthday candles, her lips in a neat kiss towards the camera.

I loved you so much. I hope you knew that, even after we'd broken up. And there are so many things I wish I could've said to you. How incredible some of our time together had been. How grateful I was to you for filling my youth with your exuberance and light. Even how often I imagined your future with someone else and a tribe of beautiful, hyperactive children. I wanted you to always stay in the spotlight because it suited you. Oh, how it suited you. And, after that last meeting of ours, I did think we would remain friends, in some way. I thought I'd read about you—reviews of your performances, perhaps—and feel a kind of pride. I had never imagined reading about you in the way that I have in these past months—in bite-size summaries of your character, in the past tense, in commemorative Australian language.

There are thousands of unfound people from that disaster, including you. I know that that is so terrible in many ways, for your family. But I also like to imagine you at the bottom of the sea somewhere. I try only to imagine you asleep—in a softer place than on land where your body would be so still: torn and broken and dry. I try only to imagine you in a gentle sleep.

On the day Ana Poulos arrived at the Centre to retrieve the panel, it was very difficult to let it go.

'Would you mind if I researched it?' I asked her.

'Researched it?'

'Yes. With the information we have about the materials and the signature, I think there's enough to do a full provenance search.'

I'd already discussed it with Gillian; she was keen to support the proposal, even suggesting that the project could be the Centre's submission for an international scheme. I was pleased with her enthusiasm, but aware of the inevitable problem with Joy; she'd tried for the last two years to lead a successful application. I was already considering approaches to distill the conflict between us.

'Really?' said Mrs Poulos. 'You think it's worth studying?'

'Definitely. I should be able to get some leave, travel, find some money from somewhere to fund it. There's got to be a good story behind this painting.'

'Caterina's story?'

'And yours. And whoever else has been looking after it for five centuries.'

'Where will you start?' she asked.

'Probably with the pigment. There might be workshop records, guild records. There's definitely something suspect about an inexperienced artist with that much ultramarine.'

'Yes,' she agreed. 'Keep me informed, won't you?'

'Of course,' I said quietly.

'Have you thought about it much?' Mrs Poulos asked, waving her hand towards the wrapped painting on the laminate table.

'The panel?'

'Yes. Have you imagined anything?'

'Yes,' I said, suppressing my surprise. 'I've thought about it *constantly*. I've imagined a whole saga involving Caterina and her family and a gentleman on his Grand Tour and a ballerina in Paris and migration. Lots of water, loss, love stories.'

'Well, why do the research then?' she said. 'The real story might not be so good.'

That's true, I thought. It might not. Or it could be better.

Mrs Poulos picked up the parcel I'd prepared: the panel and its folder of documentation.

As she walked towards the exit door, she was saying thank-yous to me that I wasn't hearing properly. Why did I want to find out about this artwork when I had my own ideas already? But that was like asking, why love when you can read a romance novel? Same logic. Same cynicism.

'Katerina?' Mrs Poulos said.

'Yes?' I answered, turning to her.

'Good luck.'

And that was it. She left the Centre with a pair of angels on a piece of poplar.

A couple of months later, I got my research grant.

And I came here to Venice to find the answer to a story.

Acknowledgements

Thank you to Fiona Hazard, Robert Watkins, and everyone at Hachette for republishing this novel, and Alissa Dinallo for the beautiful cover.

Thank you to Clare Forster for her belief and commitment over so many years.

Thank you to the original team at Allen & Unwin, and the judges and trustees of the Miles Franklin Literary Award and the Dobbie Literary Award for the recognition.

For support, advice and readings throughout the writing process of *Fugitive Blue*, I am grateful to Chris and Cheryl Thomas, George Papaellinas, Katie Ridsdale, the staff of the Ian Potter Centre for Art Conservation and the School of Culture and Communication at the University of Melbourne, Tony Birch, Sam Brown, Marion M. Campbell, Annette Hughes,

Sue Booth-Forbes, Ari Hatzis, Alison Huber, Annabelle Roxon and Rachel Mudge.

My daughter, Camille, was two weeks old at the launch of *Fugitive Blue* and now she has just started secondary school. Thank you, my darling girl, for being my treasure.

To Leo, Gus and Andy – thank you for arriving later, full of love.

This novel was written, with gratitude, admiration and respect, on the land of the Wurundjeri People of the Kulin Nation. Always was, always will be, Aboriginal land.

ALSO BY CLAIRE THOMAS

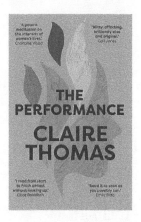

The false cold of the theatre makes it hard to imagine the heavy wind outside in the real world, the ash air pressing onto the city from the nearby hills where bushfires are taking hold.

The house lights lower.

The auditorium feels hopeful in the darkness.

As bushfires rage outside the city, three women watch a performance of a Beckett play.

Margot is a successful professor, preoccupied by her fraught relationship with her ailing husband. Ivy is a philanthropist with a troubled past, distracted by the snoring man beside her. Summer is a young theatre usher, anxious about the safety of her girlfriend in the fire zone.

As the performance unfolds, so does each woman's story. By the time the curtain falls, they will all have a new understanding of the world beyond the stage.

'Witty, affecting, brilliantly wise and original.' GAIL JONES

'A potent meditation on the intensity of women's lives.'
CHARLOTTE WOOD

'I read from start to finish almost without looking up.'
CLARE BOWDITCH

hachette
AUSTRALIA

If you would like to find out more about Hachette Australia,
our authors, upcoming events and new releases you can visit
our website or our social media channels:

hachette.com.au

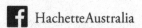 HachetteAustralia

 HachetteAus